SKELETON CREW

Slowly Joe walked along the rocking deck. He had one hand on the rail and the other on his torch.

The boat lurched in the water, and Joe lost his balance, waving the torch awkwardly in the direction of the wheelhouse. The flame cast an eerie light, but he had no difficulty picking out the figure at the wheel of the ship.

It was a man, or what remained of a man.

The body was nothing but a skeleton frozen in time.

Books in THE HARDY BOYS CASEFILES® Series

Available from ARCHWAY Paperbacks

THE DEAD SEASON

FRANKLIN W. DIXON

AN ARCHWAY PAPERBACK
Published by POCKET BOOKS
New York   London   Toronto   Sydney   Tokyo

AN ARCHWAY PAPERBACK *Original*

An Archway Paperback published by
POCKET BOOKS, a division of Simon & Schuster Inc.
1230 Avenue of the Americas, New York, NY 10020

ISBN: 0-671-67483-8

First Archway Paperback Printing January 1990

10 9 8 7 6 5 4 3 2 1

Printed in the U.S.A.

IL 7+

THE DEAD SEASON

Chapter

1

"BUT YOU'RE THE FOURTH cab driver we've asked," Callie Shaw said in desperation. "Why won't anyone take us to Runner's Harbor?"

"I don't know about anybody, but I'm on my break," mumbled the cabbie.

"Doesn't anybody around here work for a living?" grumbled Joe Hardy.

Frank Hardy pointed toward a battered black cab parked in the shade of a huge palm tree a couple hundred feet away. "There's another one."

Again they picked up their luggage and trudged wearily beneath the late-afternoon sun. The air was damp and made their walk uncomfortable.

"Boy, is it hot," said Joe, pausing a moment to push a strand of blond hair off his forehead.

1

Sweat was once again running into his eyes, making them sting.

"It'll be cool at the hotel," said Callie, her enthusiasm still high. "My cousin Gary says it's always pleasant there."

"Speaking of your cousin," said Joe, "why didn't he meet us at the airport?"

"I told you," Callie said, just keeping the exasperation out of her voice. "He and his wife, Janet, are both too busy running things at the hotel."

Joe shook his head. "Maybe I should have stayed home in nice, cool Bayport. This trip was a bad idea from the start. You and Frank would have had more fun alone, anyway."

"Oh, Joe!" cried Callie. "You've been griping ever since we left. I don't know how you can be so gloomy about a nice tropical vacation."

She was right, and Joe knew it. But who could blame him? Spending all this time with Frank and Callie made him feel like a third wheel. He had insisted he'd be in the way, but Frank and Callie begged him to come.

Callie insisted, "We want you here, Joe. Don't we, Frank?"

"Of course we do," said Frank.

Joe thought for a moment and then grinned. "Well, all right," he said. "Let the vacation begin." Frank and Joe's father, Fenton Hardy, had been the one to talk Joe into taking the trip.

"Believe me," Fenton Hardy had said, "I know how difficult your last investigation was. Take the vacation. You've earned it. It'll do you good."

The trio had arrived in Barbados about an hour earlier and had no trouble getting their luggage and making their way out of the airport to the taxi stand. Their problems started when they had tried to get a ride to Runner's Harbor. All of the cabbies they approached had turned down their requests to take them to the hotel.

Frank set his bags down for a second to whistle and wave at the old taxi driver, who was still leaning against his dented cab.

The man saw them, smiled, and waved back. Frank hustled along behind his brother and Callie.

Frank, the elder of the two brothers, was taller and leaner than Joe and had dark hair and eyes. Maybe it was because he was older, or maybe it was because he was more thoughtful than Joe, but Frank always seemed to take things a little easier.

"Good afternoon," said Frank to the slender old man, who seemed not to have a care in the world. His cab was a huge black Buick that Frank guessed was of late twenties' vintage, the sort of car that gangsters drove during Prohibition.

"That it is," said the old man.

"Can you take us to Runner's Harbor?" asked Frank hopefully.

"For twenty dollars I will take you anywhere on the island of Barbados," he answered.

"Twenty dollars!" exclaimed Joe.

"We'll take it," said Frank.

Joe gave his brother a look but said nothing more, and the three of them put their luggage in the trunk of the old cab and climbed in. Joe got in the front next to the driver. Frank climbed in the back, directly behind the driver, and Callie sat beside him. Before the old man started the motor, he said quietly, "That would be in advance."

Again Joe started to say something, but he stopped himself. Frank paid the man and they were off.

The drive took them along the coast highway. Even Joe found himself relaxing as he took in the sweeping view of the Atlantic. The landscape out the opposite window was lush with dense green vegetation and countless brightly colored tropical flowers. The air was laced with the distinctive salty smell of the sea, and a cool breeze wafted over them.

"How far is it to Runner's Harbor?" asked Callie.

"Ten miles as the crow flies," said the driver, "but seeing as we ain't crows, we should be there in about twenty minutes or so." The driver paused a moment and then said, "Why is it that

4

three nice people like you are going to Runner's Harbor?"

Callie said, "My cousin and his wife own it and invited us to spend a week there as their guests. Do you know them? Gary and Janet Shaw?"

"No, miss, can't say as I do."

"Why wouldn't any of the other taxi drivers take us out to Runner's Harbor?" Callie asked. "Is it too far or something?"

"They were afraid," answered the driver.

"Afraid?" said Joe.

"Afraid of what?" asked Frank.

"Runner's Harbor is haunted," said the driver.

"Haunted?" said Joe. "There's no such thing as ghosts."

"Perhaps," said the driver.

Callie turned to Frank. "Gary never said anything about ghosts."

"Perhaps he didn't wish to frighten you," the driver replied.

"Why do you say Runner's Harbor is haunted?" asked Frank.

"Many bad things have happened there."

"What kind of bad things?" Joe asked.

"People go there and never return."

"But Gary would have told me if there was anything wrong," Callie insisted.

"What exactly did he tell you?" Joe asked.

Callie furrowed her brow as she tried to remember the letter. "He said that he and Janet hadn't seen me since I was a little girl and that he thought it would be a great idea if I visited. He added that I could invite some friends if I wanted.''

"And you chose us." Joe sighed.

"Of course," she said.

"How long have Gary and Janet owned Runner's Harbor?" Frank asked Callie.

"Two years."

To the driver Frank said, "How long have bad things been happening there?"

The driver said, "They started the day Wiley Reed disappeared."

"Who is Wiley Reed?" asked Callie.

"He built Runner's Harbor," said the driver. "It wasn't always a hotel. It started out as Wiley's private estate."

"He must have been rich," said Callie.

"That he was," said the old man, a hint of fondness creeping into his voice. "Wiley Reed was as rich as you'd want to be. Made his fortune selling rum in the States when that wasn't exactly legal, if you know what I mean."

"He was a bootlegger," said Frank.

"The best," said the driver.

"And when did he disappear?" asked Joe.

"That would be in 1929," the driver continued. "Wiley Reed had fallen in love and married, and was about to become a father. He was going to make one last run, returning in time for the birth

6

of his baby. He aimed to settle down and be respectable then,'' said the old man. "Goodness knows he'd made enough money by then to pull it off.''

"How do you know so much?'' asked Joe.

"You live as long as I have, you pick things up.''

"What happened to the wife and her baby?'' asked Callie.

"Millicent? Oh, she had a little boy. They lived out on the estate for a while, but she didn't have much heart for it. Years passed and Wiley was never seen or heard from again. She died of a broken heart, I think, before her son turned seven.''

"That's so sad,'' said Callie.

"It is,'' the old man agreed. "And now Wiley's and Millicent's ghosts wander the grounds at Runner's Harbor, searching for each other.''

"There's no such thing as ghosts,'' scoffed Joe.

"Have it your way,'' said the driver.

"What about the son?'' asked Frank.

"He's married and still lives on the island. He works at the Tyler Inn, down the beach from Runner's Harbor.''

"Not *at* Runner's Harbor?'' said Callie.

"Nope. He owned that once but lost it years ago.''

"How?'' asked Joe.

"That I don't know,'' the driver said.

7

The driver didn't say another word until the huge old car nosed its way into the gates at Runner's Harbor. "Far as I go," he said, pulling the cab to a halt.

"You said you'd take us to Runner's Harbor," Joe complained.

"And I did."

It was obvious that nothing would change his mind, so the three of them climbed out of the car, retrieved their luggage from the trunk, and watched as the taxi backed out of the driveway before speeding away. When it was gone they turned and for the first time considered the road to Runner's Harbor.

The sun was setting and the sky was a brilliant red. The thick canopy of palm trees that covered the drive made the walk to Runner's Harbor dark and ominous.

They trudged along with their heavy suitcases until Callie stopped abruptly. "What's that?" she whispered anxiously.

"What's what?" demanded Joe.

"I heard something," she insisted.

"It's nothing," Frank told her.

They moved on through the dense foliage. Then Callie put her suitcase down and said, "There it is again."

"I heard it, too," said Joe.

They paused and listened. At first they heard

nothing but the distant roar of the ocean and the rustle of the palm fronds stirring in the wind.

Then a man popped out from the shadows of the underbrush. He was dressed in an outdated navy blue suit with silver pinstripes and wide lapels. His head was covered with a broad-brimmed hat that cast a dark shadow over the place where his face should have been. But he had no face. In its place was nothing, just a black void.

He was holding a pistol in his right hand, and he slowly raised it, aiming it straight at them.

Chapter
2

As QUICKLY AS THE APPARITION had appeared, it was gone.

The Hardys and Callie stared openmouthed at the thick green foliage, but there was no more sign of the man in the thick jungle undergrowth.

"What was that?" gasped Callie.

"I haven't a clue," said Joe, struggling with the thought that he had just seen a ghost.

"Me, either," said Frank.

Quickly Joe dropped his bags and said, "I'm going to check it out."

"I'm not sure that's such a good idea," said Frank.

"Why not?" asked Joe.

"Two reasons. One, this is his turf, whoever or whatever we saw," said Frank.

"Second?"

"He had a gun."

Joe thought for a moment and picked up the bags he had dropped. "Good enough for me," he said. "Let's get to the hotel."

"Good idea," Frank agreed, and the trio hurried up the driveway to Runner's Harbor.

In another three hundred feet the driveway opened up onto a large grass-covered hill. At the very top of the hill sat Runner's Harbor, and beyond it was the Atlantic Ocean, flame colored from the setting sun. The hotel was an immense structure of clapboard and brick that had clearly seen better days. The shingle roof sagged, and the paint was losing its battle with the salt air. Still, there was something inviting about the place. The building offered a warm welcome.

With the hotel now in sight, the Hardys and Callie walked faster.

"It's wonderful," said Callie. "Oh, Frank. Don't you think it's wonderful?"

Joe was about to make a wisecrack about the condition of the hotel when he heard his brother say enthusiastically, "I do. It's great. Don't you think so, Joe?"

"Yeah, sure," mumbled Joe.

As they stepped onto the wide front porch, the double doors to the entrance opened and a man and woman stepped outside. They hurried to give Callie a hug.

"Callie!" said the woman. "It's been ages."

Callie blushed at the attention, took a step back, and said, "Frank and Joe Hardy, this is my cousin Gary Shaw and his wife, Janet. Gary and Janet, this is Frank and Joe Hardy."

"We've heard so much about both of you," said Gary.

"Likewise," said Frank as he shook Gary's hand.

Gary and Janet both had ready smiles, large brown eyes, and close-cropped hair, but there the similarities ended. Gary was tall, slender, red-headed, and fair skinned and seemed to be nursing a bad sunburn. Janet was plump and short with dark hair and an olive complexion.

"How was your trip?" asked Janet as she and Gary guided the travelers inside.

"Okay, until we got to the airport," answered Callie. She explained what had happened up to and including the incident with the Ghost Gunman.

"Not again," Janet said with a sigh.

Frank said, "You mean the Ghost Gunman has been seen before?"

"A few times, actually," said Gary.

"But no one has ever been hurt," said Janet quickly.

"You mean your hotel *is* haunted?" asked Callie.

"I wouldn't say that," said Gary, a bit defensively.

"What would you say?" asked Joe.

Janet said, "Runner's Harbor has a very rich history. The man who built it, Wiley Reed, was a living legend around here."

"Our cab driver told us a little about him," said Frank.

Gary continued. "Wiley Reed vanished in the twenties, and they never found his body. The locals cooked up this ghost thing, but if you ask me, it's just the product of overactive imaginations."

"That wasn't my imagination out there today," said Joe.

"Mine, either," said Callie.

"When did you first see this Ghost Gunman?" asked Frank.

"We're being terrible hosts," said Janet, obviously interrupting the conversation. "Gary can answer your questions, but let's do it while we show you your rooms."

They walked through the heavy glass- and walnut-paneled doors, across the spanking clean lobby, and up the sweeping dark wood staircase that dominated it. "Your rooms are on the second floor. I hope you like them," said Janet.

Gary said, "Janet and I have never actually seen the Ghost Gunman, but people who've stayed here have seen him—ever since we bought the place."

"That was two years ago?"Frank asked.

"Uh-huh," Gary replied.

They had come to a landing where the staircase split into two sets of stairs. A larger-than-life oil painting, the portrait of a beautiful woman in her midtwenties, dominated the landing. The woman in the painting had intense green eyes and shoulder-length auburn hair. She was wearing what looked like a white wedding gown. Around her throat was a beautiful ruby pendant. She also wore large diamond earrings and a matching diamond bracelet.

"Who's that?" Joe asked.

"Isn't she beautiful? That's Millicent Reed," Janet told them. "Wiley Reed's wife."

"She's more than beautiful," Joe whispered.

"She's gorgeous," said Callie. "What exactly happened to her? Our cab driver told us she died of a broken heart."

"She died many years ago," Gary explained.

"It's so sad," said Callie.

"Isn't it?" Janet agreed.

They all gazed at the painting for a moment longer and then, wordlessly, picked up the suitcases and continued walking up the stairs.

"What do you think happened to Wiley?" asked Frank.

"Well," said Gary, "there are two theories.

One says that Wiley wanted to disappear. But that doesn't make much sense. Everything I ever heard about him says he loved Millicent and this place. Why would he want to leave?"

"And the other theory?" asked Joe.

"That someone murdered him."

"Murder!" said Callie. "But who, and why?"

"The who is probably something we'll never know," said Gary. "And as to the why, Wiley was a very rich man who was involved with some pretty dangerous people."

"The mob," started Frank.

"Right," Gary said, nodding. "Running rum was perfectly legal here on the islands, but it was very much against the law in the States during Prohibition."

They were on the second floor, and Janet brought them to a halt in front of a door marked 201. "This will be Callie's room. We've put Frank in two-oh-two and Joe in two-oh-three. How's that?"

"Great," said the Hardys and Callie in unison.

Janet smiled. "Why don't you settle in, and Gary can finish his ghost stories at dinner."

"More coffee, anyone?" asked Janet as she walked around the Runner's Harbor dining room carrying a pot of fresh-brewed coffee.

"Yes, thank you," said Allistair Gaines, the

15

oldest resident at the hotel both in terms of age and of time spent there.

Frank and Callie had quickly unpacked so they could take advantage of the magnificent sunset on the beach. Joe had wandered around and checked out the large half-sided pavilion near the beach, the dilapidated boathouse, and a small shed.

Before dinner Gary and Janet had introduced the Hardys and Callie to the other guests. It had not taken long since there were only four others.

By the time dinner came they were very hungry, and Janet had proved herself to be a very good chef. Only Joe had found room for dessert.

As he watched Janet pour coffee, Frank considered what Gary had told them about the other guests at the hotel.

Gaines, a man in his late seventies or early eighties, had lived on the island most of his life. He was a melancholy man with flowing white hair and a long white mustache. He wore what had been expensive clothes that were now showing their age, but the most striking thing about him was his jewelry. He wore several large rings and had gold cufflinks and a gold tie clip in the shape of a large letter *G*.

Earl Logan had lived at the hotel for several weeks, but not much was known about him. A sullen man in his late forties or early fifties, he was nondescript in almost every way. His skin was pale, and his greasy blond hair was parted sloppily on one side. Frank noticed a small tattoo on Logan's right hand, a crudely drawn skull and crossbones on the fleshy skin between his thumb and index finger. The only other thing about him that was noteworthy was the lit cigarette he always had dangling from his lips.

The last two guests were the Wilkersons, Paul and Denise, a young couple in Barbados for their honeymoon. They were both blond, slender, and athletic looking. Although they were friendly enough, they obviously wanted their privacy.

Not long after dinner the Hardys and Callie excused themselves and said good night.

After the long trip all they wanted was to go to bed and get a good night's sleep. There would be time enough the next day to sightsee and hear all of Gary's ghost stories.

In the hallway outside their rooms Frank said, "I thought I was the only one who was exhausted."

"No," said Callie with a yawn and a shake of her head. "Good night."

"Must be the salt air," said Joe.

"Good night," said Frank. "See you in the morning."

"Happy vacation," said Callie, and gave Frank a quick good-night kiss on the cheek.

*　　*　　*

A cool ocean breeze wafted in through the open window in Frank's room. When he first heard the screams, he thought they were coming from outside.

Then he thought he was dreaming.

But now he was wide-awake, and his blood ran cold as he realized the sound was coming from inside Runner's Harbor.

It was Callie, and she was screaming for her life.

Chapter

3

FRANK RACED DOWN THE HALLWAY with Joe right behind him. Callie had stopped screaming now, and Frank feared the worst.

The room was dark when Frank and Joe pushed the door open. In the shadows they could just make out Callie standing on the bed, her back pressed against the wall.

"Watch out!" she warned in a voice hushed with fear.

"What is it?" whispered Frank.

"S-snake." Callie pointed a shaky finger at the foot of the bed.

"There." Joe nodded. He reached to turn on the light, but Frank stopped him.

"Not yet!"

Joe held back. "How should we handle it?"

"Very carefully," Frank answered quietly.

At the foot of Callie's bed was a coral snake. Even in the dim light from the hallway its colors— alternating bands of yellow, black, and red—were vivid and shimmering. The snake, which seemed to be about three feet long, was coiled into a circle and looked harmless enough.

Under his breath Joe said, "Is it poisonous?"

"If it's what I think it is—it is," whispered Frank with a nod. His lips were pursed as he tried to think of a way to capture the snake. To Callie, in a normal but soothing voice, he said, "Just stay where you are. Everything's going to be okay. Joe, when I say *now,* I want you to turn on the light."

Gary, Janet, and the Wilkersons were now gathered in the hallway at the open door.

"What's wrong?" asked Gary.

"Nothing," said Frank very quietly. "We'll handle this." He turned toward the snake.

Cautiously he approached the snake until he was standing directly over it. Very quietly he bent over and reached with his right hand for the snake's head. *"Now!"* he whispered loudly, and in the instant that the light flashed on Frank grasped the snake tightly just below its mouth and held it high, restraining its gaping mouth until he could throw it head-first into the pillowcase that Joe held out in front of him.

With a swift, sure movement, he tied the open end of the case into a firm knot.

"Done." He sighed. He turned and faced a concerned-looking Gary.

"What was that all about?" Gary asked worriedly. Frank explained the situation and that he had gotten rid of the problem.

"Is Callie okay?" Janet asked from behind Gary, trying to peer into the room.

"I'm fine," Callie called out in a shaky voice.

"Is the snake in that pillowcase?" Gary asked.

"Yes. It's an extremely poisonous coral snake, and I'm glad we got here in time," Frank said.

Seeing that everything was under control, Gary broke the group up and suggested they all return to bed.

After Frank had taken the snake outside and set it loose far from the hotel, he, Callie, and Joe took a walk on the beach to calm down after the excitement.

"What I can't figure out is how that snake got in your room," said Frank, still mulling over the night's excitement.

They might have continued talking about the snake, but at that moment they were interrupted by the muted sound of piano playing.

"Where's that coming from?" asked Frank.

"Sounds like the piano on the pavilion," said Joe, "but I can't imagine who'd be playing piano at this hour."

The pavilion was an ornate, half-open structure that was about midway between the hotel and a cliff that dropped a hundred feet or so to the beach.

Joe wrinkled his brow and said, "That song sounds familiar."

"It's by Gershwin," said Callie. " 'Someone to Watch Over Me.' " When they were about fifty feet from the pavilion, the music stopped as abruptly as it had begun.

There was no sound but the waves crashing against the rocks farther along on the beach. Light from a nearly full moon cast long shadows across the pavilion dance floor, and at the far end of the floor was the piano.

No one was in sight. Joe and Callie walked around the pavilion quietly and found nothing.

"I wonder who was playing," said Frank.

"It was lovely," said Callie.

The three of them stood in silence for a moment. Finally Frank said, "Why would someone play the piano in the middle of the night?" They left and made a surveillance tour of as much of the grounds as they could in the dim light but found nothing.

As the three of them walked back, they passed a section of the hotel that was in the midst of being repaired. Prominently placed on one wall was a sign that said, "Renovation by Tyler Construction. Barbados's Oldest Building Company."

Frank paused a moment to read it, and Joe said, "What do you think?"

"Maybe someone on the construction crew knows what's happening around here. It's as close to a lead as we've got," said Frank. "We'll check it out with the company in the morning."

The rest of that night passed uneventfully, but in the morning, when the Hardys went downstairs, they found the Wilkersons checking out of the hotel. Paul was explaining to Janet that Denise was terrified of snakes and they didn't feel they'd be able to enjoy the rest of their honeymoon. They apologized, then left.

After breakfast Callie went sightseeing with Janet and Gary, and Joe and Frank borrowed one of the hotel's cars and paid a visit to Tyler Construction, which was about five miles down the coast road from Runner's Harbor. The building that housed the company was a modest but attractive white brick structure nestled under palm trees.

As Frank and Joe walked from the car through the small parking lot to the entrance, Joe asked, "Just what are we looking for here? Snake handlers or guys in suits from the 1920s who knew Al Capone?"

"Very funny," said Frank. "I don't know, but

Tyler's men have been working around the hotel for some time, and maybe one of them's seen something. It's worth checking out. We won't stay long. Then we'll go back and hit the beach, okay?'' Joe nodded his consent.

A receptionist in the cool office showed the Hardys into a larger one. A large wooden ceiling fan circulated the air gently.

A tall, tanned man stood up from behind a polished mahogany desk and said, ''Randolph Tyler. Pleased to meet you. How can I be of service?''

''I'm Frank Hardy. This is my brother, Joe. We're staying at Runner's Harbor, and we wanted to ask you a few questions.''

They all shook hands. From a corner of the room a young man appeared. He was perhaps a year or two older than Frank. Slender and dark haired, he wore wire-rimmed glasses that framed sullen brown eyes.

''Sorry to interrupt,'' he said to the boys, ''but Mr. Tyler's time is very short.''

Tyler looked at the young man curiously, then turned to Frank and Joe and said, ''Brady's right, as usual. This is Brady Jamison, my assistant.''

To the Hardys Jamison said, ''Can these questions wait? I'm afraid we really have to go shortly, and I don't believe you had an appointment.''

Joe fought an urge to say something rude to

Jamison but instead told Tyler, "We can be very brief."

"That seems reasonable to me," said Tyler. "Have a seat. We've got a few minutes."

The Hardys took chairs in front of Tyler's desk as Brady Jamison mumbled, "Only a few."

"What can I tell you?" asked Tyler.

"This is a bit strange, I know," said Frank, "but we were wondering what you could tell us about Runner's Harbor."

Brady Jamison interrupted to say snidely, "I'm sure you can find all the answers to those questions at the Barbados Public Library. It's really very well stocked with history books. All about the exploits of the very colorful criminal Wiley Reed."

"That's enough, Brady." Randolph Tyler smiled at his assistant with a patience that seemed well practiced. He turned his attention back to Frank and Joe. "Brady's dad and I were partners, so Brady and I go way back." He smiled at the young man again. "My family has lived on this island for five generations. There's very little I don't know. Briefly, Runner's Harbor was built by Wiley Reed in the twenties and was his base of operations for a very lucrative rum-exporting business. Shipping liquor *out* of Barbados was not illegal. What he did with it on the other end was of no concern to people here. He did very well, I understand. Now, my company has been hired to renovate the place. I own the hotel you drove by to get here, and adding Runner's Harbor and all its property to my hotel would make it the finest and largest resort in the Caribbean. I hope to buy it someday."

"Why didn't you buy it?" asked Frank. "Gary and Janet just got it two years ago."

"That's really none of your business," Brady Jamison interrupted again. "What's this all about?"

Tyler considered Frank a moment and said, "Brady may be blunt, but he has a point. You haven't told us why you're asking all these questions."

Frank told Tyler who they were, that he and Joe and Callie were visiting Callie's cousin, and that there were some unexplained occurrences at the hotel, and they just wanted to ask some questions.

"What sort of things?" asked Tyler.

"Well," Frank began, "someone put a coral snake in one of the guest rooms last night."

"The island is full of snakes, I'm afraid," Tyler offered, "and with all the digging we've been doing, it's no surprise that one could turn up in a room. Now, what else?"

Brady Jamison abruptly ended the meeting right then by insisting that he and Tyler leave for their appointment.

The four of them walked to the parking lot together.

As he prepared to get into his jeep, Tyler turned to the Hardys and said, "A word of friendly advice?"

"Sure," said Frank.

"I think you boys should relax and enjoy the island and not get caught up in local nonsense. Lie on the beach and take it easy."

The Hardys took his advice. Soon after their meeting with Tyler and Brady Jamison, they were stretched out on the white sandy beach, lazing beneath the warm sun. Huge blue waves folded over on themselves and slid up on the sand to keep them company.

Late in the afternoon Callie joined them. Finally at sunset they strolled back to the hotel to eat too much of Gary and Janet's special supper.

Afterward they sat on the huge porch enjoying the cool night air. Lulled by the gentle sounds of the ocean, they went to bed early.

Joe had trouble sleeping. He'd spent too much time dozing on the beach to need more sleep.

For a long time he lay in bed tossing and turning. No matter what he did, he couldn't sleep.

"This is ridiculous," he mumbled to himself.

Around midnight he decided to get some fresh air. A walk on the beach might make him drowsy, he decided.

Joe got out of bed, pulled on his jeans and a shirt, and was about to leave his room when something out the window caught his eye.

Down the hill he spotted someone walking on the beach.

Joe went to the open window and looked at the distant figure lit by the moon.

"This can't be," he whispered.

It was Millicent Reed.

Chapter

4

IT COULDN'T BE MILLICENT REED, but it was.

Joe had to get to the beach. He had to convince himself one way or another. He had to put this ghost business to rest.

Glancing at the door, he decided there wasn't time for the stairs, so he took the direct route.

Joe crawled out the window and scrambled down a vine that reached from his window to the ground, then ran down the hill to the beach.

He calculated that from the time he first spotted Millicent Reed to the time he reached the beach was no more than two minutes, but by the time he got there she was gone. He found the place where he had seen her and looked for footprints, but the tide was coming in now. Even if she had been there, her footprints would have been washed away.

He asked himself why he had thought "even if." There had to have been someone. He did see someone, and he knew there was no such thing as ghosts.

To be certain, Joe walked up and down the beach, but in the dim moonlight he found no clues and no place where she could have hidden. He finally decided to resume his search in the morning, so he headed back to the hotel and his bed.

Frank and Callie were already at breakfast the next morning when Joe arrived.

"Well, little brother," teased Frank. "Never knew you to be a sleepy-head. I guess the sea air agrees with you."

"Nope," Joe said. "I wish it did put me to sleep. Then I wouldn't have been up all night chasing Millicent Reed."

"What?" Callie exclaimed.

"Start at the beginning," Frank said in a quiet voice.

Between bites of scrambled egg and toast, Joe told his story about seeing the woman—Millicent Reed—on the beach. He recounted his fruitless midnight chase.

"But where could she have gone?" asked Callie.

"The tide washed any footprints away," guessed Frank.

"That's what I figured," Joe agreed. "Unless, of course—"

"Of course what?"

"Unless I saw a ghost."

"A ghost!" scoffed Frank. "Come on."

"I hate to say it, but it seemed so real," said Joe.

"But who would want to play a prank like that?" asked Callie.

"That," said Frank, "is something we have to find out. Listen, Joe. You go back to the beach this morning and see what you can find. Callie and I'll check out the rest of the grounds. Let's hope we can wrap this up by lunchtime and then start to relax."

"Sounds good to me," said Joe.

"Okay, then," said Frank. "Callie, let's go."

After they left, Joe quickly finished eating his breakfast and returned to the beach to try to retrace his steps of the night before. Even in the bright Caribbean sunlight he could see nothing that even vaguely resembled a clue. Still, he told himself as he slowly wandered along the edge of the water, there were worse places to carry out an investigation.

Perhaps a quarter mile down the beach he spotted a solitary figure sitting on a beach chair in front of a painter's easel. Even from a distance he could tell that it was Allistair Gaines.

As Joe approached it struck him that Gaines had been curiously absent when they'd found the snake in Callie's room.

"Haven't seen much of you around the hotel," said Joe, approaching the elderly man.

"True, true," said Gaines without looking away from his painting. "Stay to myself pretty much. Pretty much to myself. Always been that way. Always."

Joe thought a moment before saying, "Do you ever hear piano playing in the middle of the night?"

"Of course," said Gaines, still concentrating on his work. "Hear it all the time."

"You do?" Joe was incredulous. "Any idea who's playing?"

"I got more than ideas, son," said Gaines, looking at Joe for the first time. "I know perfectly well who it is."

"Who?"

"Wiley, of course." Gaines looked back to his painting.

"How do you know it's him?" Joe asked.

"Millicent told me."

Joe wasn't sure whether to pursue this or just let it go. Allistair Gaines was clearly of no help to him.

"By any chance, were you on the beach last night, say around midnight?" asked Joe.

"Sound asleep," said Gaines. "Sound asleep. Man needs his rest. Why? Did you see Millicent?"

"How did you know?" Joe asked.

Gaines just smiled and tilted his head.

"Well," said Joe, "when did you see Millicent?"

"See her all the time, son, all the time," said the old man, with a trace of annoyance in his voice now. "She often comes out at night to stroll on the beach. Once in a while you'll see her during the day. Mostly at night, though. Mostly at night."

"I don't want to seem rude, Mr. Gaines," Joe began, sensing the man was running out of patience, "but hasn't Millicent Reed been dead for many years?"

Gaines let his brush fall away from the canvas but continued to gaze at his painting. In a hoarse, quiet voice he said, "Of course."

"Then—"

"Then who does a crazy old man think he's talking to?"

Joe didn't say anything.

"I'll tell you, I never believed in ghosts till I came back to this hotel, but that's Millicent I saw, sure as I'm sitting here."

Joe said, "When did you see her last?"

"Maybe five minutes ago."

"Five minutes!" said Joe. "Where?"

"Here," said Gaines with a dismissive wave of his hand. He picked up his brush, dipped it carefully into a splotch of white on his palette, and resumed his work.

"Which way did she go?" asked Joe.

Gaines nodded with his head to indicate farther along the beach. "Thanks!" Joe called out as he started in that direction.

He found footprints about fifty feet from where Gaines was sitting. They formed a line along the edge of the water that was interrupted in a few places where the waves had erased it.

Joe walked faster now; he didn't want to lose the trail.

He needn't have worried.

Perhaps a hundred yards ahead he could see where the footprints stopped. There, apparently asleep on a blanket, a woman was sunbathing.

Joe's heart raced inexplicably as he hurried to where she lay.

What if it really is Millicent? he asked himself. But, of course, it isn't, he thought. There's no such thing as a ghost, especially on a beach in broad daylight.

"Hello," he said when he came within earshot of the woman, but she didn't respond. He moved closer.

She seemed to be about eighteen, and Joe could

see at once why Allistair Gaines or anyone would believe that she was Millicent Reed. Her long hair was the same rich red and her features were identical to those in the portrait. Her black bikini flattered her slender figure. Even Joe found it hard not to believe he had discovered Millicent Reed.

"Who are you?" he asked.

"Is that how you always greet people?" she asked as she opened her eyes and sat up on the blanket.

"Er, no," said Joe, a bit flustered.

She had the same beautiful green eyes as the woman in the portrait, and those eyes gazed directly at Joe. Her smile was friendly and warm.

"I'm, er, Joe Hardy."

Now she stood up and reached out to shake Joe's hand. "Pleased to meet you, Joe Hardy. I'm Heather Reed."

"Heather Reed."

"Is something wrong?"

"Are you any relation to Millicent Reed?"

"I'm her granddaughter. Why?"

"The resemblance."

"That's what everyone says," said Heather, sitting back down. She patted the blanket next to her. "Have a seat."

"Thanks," said Joe. He waited a second before asking his next question, but then said, "Were

35

you strolling on the beach last night around midnight?''

"Me? No. Why do you ask?"

"No reason," said Joe.

"You saw Millicent, didn't you?" asked Heather.

"I saw something," Joe said, nodding. He wasn't certain what to think about anything. He instinctively believed Heather when she said she hadn't been on the beach the night before. But what had he seen? He needed to talk it over with Frank.

At that moment Frank was almost as frustrated by events as his brother was.

Frank and Callie had spent the morning searching the grounds around Runner's Harbor and turned up nothing. Absolutely nothing.

"Let's take a break, Frank," said Callie as they approached the wide porch on the back of the hotel. It was every bit as weathered as the hotel itself. Still, the benches were comfortable, and the breeze and the magnificent view made it pleasant.

Frank guided Callie up the porch steps and took a seat next to her on a bench. "What a waste of a morning," he said.

"I guess so," said Callie, "but at least we've checked out the grounds."

"I just keep thinking that there's something we've overlooked," said Frank.

"Like what?"

Frank stood up and walked across the porch and leaned against the railing, pondering what they had seen that morning. He wrapped his fingers around a length of railing that seemed out of place.

"You haven't answered me, Frank Hardy," Callie said, and she got up from the bench and started walking toward him.

"What's this?" Frank asked himself out loud as he gave the piece of railing a tug and a trap door opened in the porch floor. Callie disappeared, swallowed up by the darkness below.

Chapter

5

"CALLIE!" FRANK SHOUTED IN ALARM. "Are you all right?"

Callie looked up at him from the bottom of the shaft, about seven feet down, where she was now sitting on a huge wooden chest.

"I—I think so," she said, "but I landed on this. It wasn't the softest thing to break my fall." She motioned weakly to the trunk.

Frank dropped down into the pit as Callie tried to stand.

"Ouch!" she cried. "I think I sprained my ankle."

"Here. Lean on me," said Frank, holding out his arm.

Callie fought back her tears. "It hurts."

"Sit down again and let me check it."

Carefully Frank inspected Callie's sore ankle. "There's no swelling," he said. "I don't think it's serious. You'll be okay. We'll get you back inside and put some ice on it. Come on."

Callie draped an arm over Frank's shoulders. As carefully as he could in the narrow space, he guided her up a ladder that was nailed to one side of the shaft. Together they walked slowly into the hotel.

Frank was in the process of treating Callie's ankle with ice and an elastic bandage when Joe walked in.

"What happened to you?" asked Joe.

"I fell," said Callie, her spirits on the rebound. "But I found, that is, we found a trap door in the porch. It led down into a shaft with a huge old wooden trunk at the bottom of it."

"Anything in the trunk?" asked Joe.

Callie and Frank exchanged a look. "We haven't looked yet," said Frank. He looked at Callie. "Maybe you should stay here and rest."

"No way," answered Callie, getting up and hopping on her good leg toward the back door. "I found that trunk the hard way and I'm going to be there when you open it."

Frank and Joe each took an arm and helped Callie walk out to the porch.

On the way Joe told them about his conversation with Allistair Gaines and about meeting Heather Reed.

"No wonder Gaines thinks he's been seeing Millicent Reed," said Joe. "It's spooky just how much Heather looks like that portrait of her grandmother."

"But she insists she wasn't on the beach last night?" asked Frank.

"Yeah," said Joe.

Callie asked, "Do you believe her?"

"I think so," Joe said. "Why would she lie?" Then he added, "But if she isn't lying, then what or who did I see on the beach last night?"

"Good question," said Frank, "and it's only one of several we have to answer."

They got to the porch and made sure Callie was seated before Joe hopped down into the pit. "It's pretty heavy," he said, lifting the trunk.

Frank reached down and took hold of a strap on the side of the trunk and pulled it out of the shaft and onto the floor of the porch.

"Front-row seat," Frank told Callie.

"Hurry up and open it," she said excitedly.

"It's jammed," said Frank as he tested the lid.

With a sharp kick Joe knocked the top loose and said, "Now it isn't."

Frank looked at his younger brother for a moment and said, "I was going to get some tools."

"Saved you a trip."

"Let's open it!" cried Callie impatiently.

Frank lifted the lid and released a cloud of musty air.

"This thing has been closed for years," he said.

One by one Frank began to remove the items in the trunk. For the most part it was filled with old clothes.

"They look like the kind of clothes that character who met us on the road was wearing," said Callie. "They must be pretty old."

At the bottom of the trunk were three very dusty bottles of rum. "I wonder if Dad would like one of these?" Joe asked.

Frank studied the now-empty trunk carefully.

"Is that everything?" asked Joe.

"Maybe," answered Frank, reaching around the bottom of the chest. "Wait a second. False bottom."

He released the catch of the false bottom and pulled out a large sheaf of papers bound by a leather strap. The papers were dry and yellow and looked as if they could crumble in Frank's hands.

When Frank undid the leather strap, he found that the papers were separated into several batches. One was a sheaf of documents stamped by the colonial government of Barbados.

"What do they say, Frank?" Callie asked from the edge of her seat.

"I want to go over these more closely," said Frank, "but they seem to cover the years 1925

41

through 1928 and, if I read them right, give Wiley Reed permission to transport rum off the island."

"It's hard to believe those papers are so old," said Callie. "It makes Wiley Reed seem almost alive."

Joe gave her a disapproving look and said, "You're beginning to sound like everyone else around here."

"Very funny," she said. "What about the rest of the papers, Frank?"

"It's hard to make out a lot of them," he said. "These, though, look like receipts for payments from Wiley to someone with the initials EBJ." He handed the documents to Joe, who studied some and passed others on to Callie.

"Excuse me," said a woman who had just walked up to them.

Callie and the Hardys were so caught up in their discovery that they didn't hear her at first, so she had to repeat herself more loudly. "Excuse me?"

Frank turned to acknowledge her. "Hello. Good morning," Frank greeted her.

"Good morning," she said in a tone that suggested it was anything but a good morning. "Could you please tell me where I can find Mr. and Mrs. Shaw?"

Callie said, "They're in the kitchen preparing lunch. Is there anything—"

"Thank you," said the woman, and she turned abruptly and walked into the hotel.

The Hardys and Callie looked at one another, quickly collected the papers, replaced the trunk, and without saying a word followed the woman.

Callie's sore ankle slowed them a bit, so that by the time they got to the kitchen much of the excitement had ended.

Once again the woman was making an abrupt exit, this time from the kitchen. "I'm afraid this is my last warning," she said. "Good day."

"What was that all about?" asked Joe.

"That was trouble," said Gary.

"Who is she?" asked Callie.

"Theresa Farr," explained Janet. "She runs the local tourist bureau and controls the licenses for all the hotels. The Wilkersons complained to her, and she's just given us our last warning."

"There've been other warnings?" asked Frank.

"A couple," answered Gary. "It took us a long time to get everything up to code, and someone reported us before we were done."

"What will you do now?" asked Frank.

"We'll just have to make certain nothing else happens," said Gary.

"What can we do to help?" asked Callie.

"Have a good time," said Janet. "This is your vacation and you should be at the beach right now."

"Janet's right," said Gary. He looked at Callie for a moment before he asked, "Why are you standing that way—as if you're about to hop off somewhere?"

Frank answered before Callie could respond. "She tripped while we were taking a walk and twisted her ankle."

"Oh, dear, is it bad?" asked Janet. "We should take you to a doctor."

"No, it's fine," muttered Callie. "I'll be okay. Really."

That afternoon the Hardys and Callie did go to the beach because they had to decide what to do next, and the beach would be a great place to talk. The three of them lay on the white sand and let the sun warm them. No one spoke. Their minds were too occupied with all they had seen.

Finally Joe broke the silence. "None of this adds up. Snakes and two ghosts and granddaughters and pianos that play themselves."

"Joe's right," said Callie. "Nothing makes sense. Are we just making things up because we love mysteries?"

"We didn't invent that snake," answered Frank. "Heather Reed is real, and we all saw that strange gunman, and we all heard the piano. I believe Joe saw Millicent."

Joe and Callie considered this, and then Callie said, "But it still doesn't make sense."

"No, it doesn't," Frank agreed, "but it will. Eventually it will—it's just we're overlooking the logical explanation."

"Why didn't you want Gary and Janet to know about the trunk?" asked Joe.

"From this point on," Frank said, "I think we should keep all the information we gather to ourselves."

"Are you saying you don't trust my cousins?" Callie asked in alarm.

"Of course not," said Frank, "but the less other people know—even people we trust—the better."

They spent the remainder of that day on the beach trying to relax, but the same questions continued to haunt them.

Frank was especially troubled, though he tried not to let Joe and Callie see it. He felt he was overlooking something, and that always bothered him.

Frank was so restless that he had difficulty falling asleep that night, and when he did, his dreams were filled with jumbled images that were confusing and made no sense.

A noise aroused him.

At first he thought it had been part of one of his dreams, but then he rolled over to discover someone in his room.

45

He almost called out, "Joe?" but stopped himself.

Frank was fully awake now and realized it wasn't his brother in his room.

It looked as if the Ghost Gunman had returned and was rifling Frank's chest of drawers.

As quietly as he could Frank eased out of bed, hoping to surprise the intruder, but the box spring squeaked and gave him away.

The Ghost Gunman turned, his face averted, and lifted a Thompson submachine gun and held it dead on Frank.

Then he squeezed the trigger!

Chapter

6

FRANK FROZE WHERE HE WAS and waited for the inevitable, but the inevitable didn't happen.

The old machine gun jammed.

The Ghost Gunman furiously squeezed the trigger time after time, but nothing happened.

Frank heard the useless clicking of the weapon's ancient workings and knew he'd been saved.

The Ghost Gunman then raised the gun like a club over his head and swung it at Frank.

Steadily Frank circled his foe, ducking the repeated blows and searching for an opening to attack himself.

The swings were coming in a regular rhythmic pattern, and Frank waited for the next upswing. Timing his leap, he knocked the gun out of the man's hand and was on top of him instantly.

The two men struggled in the darkness. As they fought, Frank told himself with certainty: This is no ghost. If he'd had any doubts before, they were gone the moment he saw the masked attacker this time. The intruder connected with a hard right cross to Frank's head.

Frank countered with a karate kick to the man's stomach. The intruder was momentarily stunned and out of breath, and Frank finished him with a quick, powerful left to the jaw.

The Ghost Gunman stumbled back and slammed into a dresser, sending a glass vase crashing to the floor.

The noise surprised both of them, and they were momentarily distracted. The gunman recovered first and picked up a lamp and smashed Frank over the head, dropping him to his knees and then onto the floor.

The Ghost Gunman picked up his submachine gun and in two strides was at the doorway. He paused, turned to Frank, and said in a low, cruel voice, "This was your last warning. Get out of Runner's Harbor."

The next thing Frank knew, he was lying in bed and Joe and Callie were hovering over him with looks of concern on their faces.

The intense searing pain in his head reminded Frank that they had some reason to be concerned.

48

"What?"

"Don't try to talk, big brother. The doctor says you'll be fine but you need to get some rest."

Callie gave Frank a glass of water. The cool water felt good. Frank ignored their advice and asked Joe, "Did you get him?"

"No," said Joe quietly. "Was it our friend in the funny clothes?"

Frank nodded a yes.

"What was he after?"

"I don't know. He did warn me, though," mumbled Frank with some difficulty. "We're supposed to leave Runner's Harbor."

"Frank," Joe said quickly, "where are those papers you and Callie found today?"

Frank could only motion to the closet. Joe crossed the room and found Frank's suitcase. In it was the bound sheaf of papers.

"I'll keep these in my room tonight," Joe said.

"Get some sleep, Frank," Callie said quietly.

"We'll talk more in the morning," Joe said.

Joe and Callie quietly stole out of the room and in seconds Frank was sound asleep.

Everyone but Allistair Gaines was at the breakfast table when Frank entered the dining room. He noticed that, as usual, Logan was sitting far from the others at the other end of the table, a sullen look on his face as he squinted through his own clouds of cigarette smoke.

It was Callie who saw Frank first. She stood up immediately and walked over to help him, scolding him all the while.

"What are you doing out of bed, Frank Hardy? You should be resting."

Easing himself into a chair, Frank grinned, then sighed. "Don't I get anything to eat?"

"I'd have brought you breakfast," said Callie. "In fact, Janet just finished making you this tray."

"Good," said Frank, pulling the napkin off the tray to reveal a huge breakfast. "I'm starved."

Frank took a long drink from a glass of freshly squeezed orange juice and then took a bite from a piece of toast.

Janet walked in then. "Judging by recent events, I guess we aren't the world's best hosts," she said, apologizing to Frank.

Before Frank could disagree, Logan muttered something under his breath and excused himself from the table.

"We've had people see Wiley's ghost before," Gary said, joining his wife, "but no one has ever been harmed."

"Something, maybe our presence here, has raised the stakes somehow," Frank said.

Frank asked, "Did anyone see Logan or Gaines around last night while I was hurt?"

"I checked last night," said Joe. "Whoever hit you may as well have vanished into thin air."

Callie said, "I saw Logan as I was running to your room. He opened his door and looked out at me. You know that sneer of his. Then he slammed his door and I forgot about him."

"Could you see what he was wearing?" asked Frank.

"Not really. It was dark and I was in a rush," answered Callie. "You think Logan hit you?"

"I don't know."

"How could Logan, or anybody, have disappeared so fast?" asked Joe.

"I may have the answer to that," said Gary. "We've never been able to find them, but the stories are that the hotel is laced with secret passages. Maybe you can find them," Gary suggested as he made his way back to the kitchen.

"Well, that's what we'll look for first," said Frank.

Right after breakfast the three began their search of the upstairs hallway.

"You'd think there'd be some sign of an opening," Joe said as he stared intently at the wallpaper for any clue that might indicate a hidden doorway.

"I sure don't see anything," agreed Callie. "A man can't just disappear. We heard your scuffle. So he'd have to go by us, but he didn't."

"Well, a man has disappeared, and more than once," said Frank. "I've got a bad feeling that we better find some answers soon."

51

Carefully they searched every inch of the hallway and all three of their rooms. They turned up nothing.

"This is getting us nowhere," said Joe, eager to do something else. "I'm no good at going over the same ground twice. This is your territory, Frank. I've got to move or I'll go nuts."

"Okay," said Frank. "You check outside and we'll keep searching in here."

The vastness of the ocean and the steady pounding of the late-morning waves helped Joe calm down, and in a few minutes the frustration he had felt inside eased. He'd left the hotel with no real plan but was formulating the bare bones of one as he walked. He had scouted the beach to the south for perhaps a mile the day he encountered Heather Reed. Now he would concentrate his attention on the beach to the north.

The beach north of the hotel was markedly different from that to the south. The south beach was basically one long stretch of white sand, but the north beach was a series of curves that formed numerous small inlets and coves.

Joe first passed the dilapidated boathouse that looked as if it hadn't been used in years. The only entrance faced the ocean, and a dock jutted out from it into the water. The rear wall was built right into a hill. It looked as if the hill was the building's only means of support.

What was that? There, inside the old boat-house, Joe saw the shadow of a man.

Joe approached quietly. Peering through a dusty window, he could just make out that the man inside appeared to be searching for something. Joe ducked beneath the window and scooted around to the dock and the only entrance to the boathouse.

"What are you doing in here?" demanded Joe fiercely.

"I—I was looking for my sunglasses," said a terrified Paul Wilkerson.

"Wilkerson?" said Joe, relaxing a little.

"There," said Wilkerson, nodding to a shelf near the entrance. "There they are." He walked to the table and picked up the sunglasses that were lying there and put them in his jacket pocket. "See you," he said, and quickly left without another word.

After Wilkerson had gone, Joe searched for clues, but there was nothing. He had all but given up and was ready to return to the hotel when a voice behind him said, "Hello."

He turned to find Heather Reed standing in the doorway.

"Hi," said Joe. "How're you?"

"Good. And you?" she asked.

"Can't complain," Joe said.

Heather asked, "What brings you to the boat-house?"

"I could ask you the same question," said Joe.

"I keep my sailboat tied up near here," Heather said with a nod toward a trim fourteen-foot sailboat that bobbed in the gentle waves nearby. "I was getting ready to sail when I saw you in here. Like to come along?"

Joe spent the rest of that day sailing with Heather. She had packed a picnic lunch, which she shared with him.

The ocean was calm and the breeze was steady, making it a perfect day for sailing.

Joe and Heather sat side by side at the rear of the boat and took turns manning the tiller. He knew enough about sailing to recognize that Heather was an expert. He told her so.

"Thanks," she said. "I love it."

They said very little but were happy just to sail in silence.

Late in the afternoon, as the sun was approaching the horizon, Heather said, "Ready to head back in yet?"

"Sure," said Joe.

With experienced moves Heather turned the sailboat about, and soon they were within sight of shore again.

"How're you doing?" she called out above the sound of the waves slapping the hull.

"Great."

Just then an explosion sounded and the main mast snapped. The huge sail flew into the ocean.

Heather screamed and lost her grip on the tiller. The explosion was small enough that neither of them was hurt, but they were both stunned.

Flames then erupted and shot out from a gaping hole in the front of the boat, and the prow began to dip deeper and deeper into the water. Thick smoke billowed up from wherever water doused the flames.

The boat was sinking fast.

Chapter

7

THE NEXT FEW MOMENTS seemed to take place in slow motion, but Joe knew that he had never acted faster in his life. His ears hummed with the aftershock of the explosive noise, but that was the least of his worries right then, because he now found himself several feet under water and caught in a harsh undertow.

Kicking and thrashing, he struggled to kick up and break the surface.

His body ached all over, but he told himself he had to fight harder. His life—and perhaps Heather's life as well—depended on it.

His lungs were burning now, and flashes of pain cut across his chest. He had to reach the surface—and soon.

Calm yourself, Joe, he told himself. Stay cool. Heather may need you.

He fought the panic that was building in him and forced himself to make slow, steady strokes. With not a moment to spare he burst to the surface and gulped in welcome mouthfuls of air.

Joe bobbed there for just a moment, trying to get his bearings. He quickly checked himself out and came to the conclusion that he was unharmed. His body ached from the impact of the blast, but he was okay.

"Heather," he said to himself. He had to find Heather.

"Heather!"

"Joe." Her voice was distant and faint.

Joe spun around in the water, but the light was fading quickly and he could see almost nothing. Here and there bits of debris floated past him.

"Joe," she called again. "Help me."

There. He saw her. She was clinging to a section of the hull that floated some fifty feet away.

"Hang on!" cried Joe as he swam to her.

She was crying and barely conscious when he reached her, but she didn't seem to be seriously hurt.

Without speaking, Joe reached his right arm across her chest and under her arm and slowly swam back to land.

Frank was on the beach, and he helped Joe the last few feet onto shore.

"I heard the explosion and came running. Are you all right?" asked Frank.

"Think so," Joe said between breaths.

"Let's get you both back to the hotel," said Frank, "and then you and I can start to piece some of this together."

Joe had just finished changing into dry clothes when there was a knock at his door.

"It's open," he said, and Frank stepped in.

"How's Heather?" asked Joe.

"She'll be okay. And you?"

"I'm all right. Did she have any idea what happened?"

"She said she didn't remember anything, but she's pretty beat up. We'll talk to her in the morning."

"She's here?"

Frank nodded. "Gary and Janet gave her a room for the night." Frank paused before saying what was on his mind. "You like her, don't you?"

Joe nodded.

"We're only here for a short time," Frank pointed out.

"Meaning?"

"Meaning, I don't want to see you get hurt."

Joe said, "Thanks for the advice, big brother. I won't."

"But—"

58

"No buts. Now let's get to work. We have a case to solve."

Frank studied his brother for a moment and then said, "Right. So tell me, what happened out there?"

Joe recounted the boat ride and then said, "This is getting serious, Frank. We've got to do something."

"I agree. I think," said Frank, "we have to return to basics—who and why. If we find out why, we'll know who. And if we know who, the why should follow. I think it's safe to assume that Gary and Janet are not responsible. I mean, they're not trying to drive themselves away from their own hotel."

"Agreed."

"Well, then," said Frank, "let's start by questioning Logan and Gaines to see if they saw or heard anything at the boathouse today."

As they walked down the hall to Logan's room, Joe suddenly remembered something.

"I can't believe I forgot this, but you know, Frank, right before Heather and I went out on her boat, I caught Paul Wilkerson snooping around the boathouse."

"What was he up to?"

"He said he had lost his sunglasses."

"Did you believe him?" asked Frank.

"Hard to say," said Joe as they reached Logan's room. "There was a pair of sunglasses there."

They had to knock several times, but finally Logan did open his door, but only a crack.

As usual, a swirl of cigarette smoke preceded him. He acknowledged their presence with a half-mumbled "Yeah?"

"Can we come in?" asked Frank.

Logan said, "No," and started to close the door, but Joe jammed his shoe against the door-frame to prevent it.

"It's okay," said Joe. "We don't need to come in. We can chat from out here."

"What do you want?"

Frank said, "There was an explosion on a boat this evening, and we were wondering if you saw or heard anything suspicious around the boat-house today."

"I didn't see nothing. I've been asleep for hours."

The Hardys waited a few seconds for Logan to volunteer something, anything, but he was clearly going to keep his mouth shut.

"Thanks for the help," said Joe sarcastically.

Allistair Gaines was not much more help, but at least he was friendly. "I'm glad you weren't hurt," he told Joe, "but I'm afraid I didn't see anything or anybody who looked suspicious. No, not me."

"Were you painting on the beach today?" asked Frank.

"Oh, of course. Of course."

"And nobody was around?"

"Just the usual people. You two and Miss Shaw and Millicent. Oh, and the construction workers."

"You saw construction workers near the beach today?" asked Joe.

"Oh, of course. I see them every day."

"When?" asked Frank.

"Time is not one of my interests," said Gaines.

The Hardys said good night to the elderly artist and decided to turn in and get an early start in the morning.

"You know, Callie's going sightseeing with Gary and Janet tomorrow," Frank said. "I'm going to spend the day at the library. There are some things in those documents we found that I want to check out. I know we decided they weren't of any interest, but now I think I have to check them out."

"What do you want me to do?"

"I'd tell you to relax and recuperate, but I know you wouldn't listen to me," said Frank.

"It runs in the family." Joe smiled. "Listen," he continued, "I'll compromise and do both. I'll take Heather and spend a nice day at the beach. We can nose around the boathouse and check it out."

*　　*　　*

True to his word, Joe slept late the next morning, and after a long and leisurely breakfast with Heather, the two of them spent the day relaxing on the beach.

Joe wished the day would not end, wished he never had to return to the States, wished there were no more mysteries to solve.

"What are you thinking?" asked Heather as they lay side by side on beach blankets.

"How good this feels," Joe answered without opening his eyes.

Around three o'clock a cool breeze picked up from out of the west, and a ridge of dark storm clouds gathered on the horizon, but Joe and Heather paid no attention to the weather.

Again it was Heather who broke the silence to say, "You remind me of my great-grandfather."

"Wiley Reed?" said Joe, turning and leaning on an elbow to look at her. "But you could never have met him."

"I didn't, but you're like what I always imagined him to be."

"I'll take that as a compliment," said Joe.

"You should."

"Have you remembered anything that might tell us who could have put the bomb on your boat?"

"Not really," she said. "I was returning it to the boathouse for the day when I saw you."

"Do you keep it at that same pier near the boathouse all the time?"

"Yes—but why?"

"I don't know. Let's take another look around to see if we can find out anything."

As they strolled in the direction of the boathouse, the gathering storm they had ignored began to grow in intensity. The wind picked up and was fierce now. As they neared the building, rain started to come down in heavy sheets.

"Hurry!" cried Joe above the sound of the storm. He put an arm around Heather to speed her along toward the boathouse.

A terrific flash of lightning that illuminated the boathouse was followed by a crack of thunder directly overhead. The boathouse looked eerie in the darkness.

There was a pause in the storm after that, and in that brief moment Joe heard another noise that stopped him dead.

"What is it?" cried Heather.

"Gunshots," said Joe. "Inside the boathouse."

Chapter

8

THE BARBADOS PUBLIC LIBRARY was small and quiet. Frank introduced himself to the librarian, told her what he wanted, and soon found himself seated in a comfortable room surrounded by stacks of local newspapers dating back to the beginning of the twenties.

The actual documents were safely hidden in Joe's suitcase, but he had jotted down notes. Wiley Reed's payments had been made to "EBJ" for a three-year period between 1925 and 1928.

"EBJ" had also initialed the official documents they had found, so Frank reasoned that this "EBJ" was a government worker and his name might appear in news accounts from that era.

The newspapers for the early years revealed nothing, but the stories they told were colorful, and Frank found it difficult to concentrate on what he had to do. Scanning an April 1925 edition, he came across the announcement of the marriage of Herbert and Madelaine Tyler. The account described a huge and lavish wedding. Frank concluded that these were Randolph Tyler's ancestors and that they were an important Barbados family as far back as the twenties.

Randolph Tyler is a powerful man, Frank thought.

There was nothing in the papers from 1925 that seemed important to Frank, but an account from an April 1926 edition caught his eye. It was the announcement that Wiley Reed and his young bride, Millicent, were building an estate called Runner's Harbor. The story described Wiley's many exploits at sea, and even in his own time, Wiley Reed was one of those rare people who was larger than life.

Later that same year, 1926, Frank came across a small review of an exhibit of oil paintings by a young artist named Allistair Gaines. The reviewer was full of praise for the work and for the artist. The writer took great pains to describe the dashing painter and all the beautiful jewelry he wore.

In 1927 there was the appointment of a new town governor, and the front page article was the information Frank had been hoping for. The new

governor's name was Elmer Bradley Jamison—
EBJ.

Frank was all but certain that Brady Jamison,
Randolph Tyler's young assistant, was related to
EBJ, but what did that mean? Would Brady Jamison have any reason to drive Gary and Janet
out of Runner's Harbor? Randolph Tyler was the
only one with a motive to do that, wasn't he?

There was nothing of interest in 1928, but a
1929 front-page article captured Frank's attention.

The headline read, "Governor Missing Five
Days."

The story was dated November 14, 1929. It
reported that no one had any idea where he might
have gone, or why, but quoted police as saying
that there was no reason to suspect foul play.

The story of Jamison's disappearance gradually lost prominence in the paper until finally a
story in January 1930 concluded that the police
had given up any hope of finding him and pre-
sumed him to be dead.

As he drove back to Runner's Harbor, Frank
tried to figure out how all the information tied
together, but none of it made sense to him. Yet.

Lost in thought, he was almost back to the
hotel when he noticed that a huge storm was
brewing on the horizon.

It was moving onshore fast.

Frank parked the jeep and hurried into the lobby just as the first fat drops began to fall.

"Hello?" he called out. "Anybody here?"

There was no answer, so Frank walked through the downstairs, checking to see if anyone was around.

"Callie? Joe? Gary? Janet?"

The only reply was a huge bolt of lightning followed by a tremendous clap of thunder.

Frank was grateful to be inside out of the storm and hoped that all the others were just as safe.

He stood at the back door and watched as the storm gathered strength.

Just then he heard gunshots.

It sounded as if they came from the direction of that old boathouse.

He grabbed a poncho from a peg on the wall beside the door and raced to the boathouse through the drenching rain.

Joe stood on the dock beside the entrance to the boathouse, but he didn't go in even though he was soaking wet and getting wetter.

There was no doubt in his mind that he had heard gunshots, and he wanted to check out the boathouse before he made a move.

He knew that if he stood in the doorway he'd be a perfect target, so he kept out of sight.

"What are you going to do?" asked Heather behind him.

Joe motioned for her to be quiet and then gestured to her to wait where she was.

Clearly she didn't like the idea, but she nodded that she understood.

With the storm raging around him, Joe said a silent prayer and, staying to the side, cautiously slipped inside the boathouse.

The only light came from the flashes of lightning that were now increasing in number.

He crouched down in a corner of the old building, and the next flash of light showed him that there, in the center of the boathouse, lay a body.

With the help of another flash of lightning, Joe made out that it was Randolph Tyler.

Another flash and he saw that Tyler had been shot in the head and was dead.

Behind him, amid the sounds of the storm, Joe heard what he thought were voices. Were they arguing?

A huge thunderclap rocked the building!

"Heather!" shouted Joe.

There was no response. In that same instant the Ghost Gunman appeared in the doorway and smashed a gun against the side of Joe's head. Joe was momentarily stunned, dropped to his knees, and found himself in several inches of water.

The storm had raised the tide and was flooding the old building.

The Ghost Gunman dashed into the dark recesses of the boathouse.

Joe could hear his footsteps as he sloshed across the ancient wooden floor.

Summoning all his strength, Joe rose to his feet.

"Heather!" he shouted. "Get help. Randolph Tyler's dead. I'm going after the gunman."

Frank raced down the hill toward the boathouse and met Heather coming the other way.

"Hurry!" she cried. "Randolph Tyler's been murdered, and Joe is chasing the killer!"

The storm seemed to have weakened a bit, but Frank suspected it was only a brief pause, that it was the eye of the storm and the worst was yet to come.

He knew he had to hurry and pushed himself to hurry even more.

Huge waves were washing into the entrance of the boathouse.

"Joe!" cried Frank. His voice seemed small in the huge space, which was rapidly filling up with water.

There was no answer.

Frank took one look at the rising water and decided he had no choice. He had to go in.

Once inside, he saw Tyler's body, now beginning to bob and float in the pulsing waves.

Again Frank had no choice.

He knew he'd have to search for Joe *after* he saw to it that the body was safe.

Frank slowly dragged Tyler's body out of the boathouse and found a relatively dry spot for it on the side of the building. Here, at least, it would not be washed out to sea.

Frank's only hope now was that the same could be said of his brother.

He ran around to the entrance of the boathouse. It was completely covered in water now.

Still, he had to go in.

He had to find Joe.

The going was incredibly difficult. The water was freezing, and his arms and legs were getting stiff in the cold.

He pushed through one step only to be pulled back toward the entrance when each wave receded.

And each new wave brought more water into the building, raising the level so it was now almost up to Frank's shoulders.

He had no idea how long it took, but he was finally at the back of the boathouse.

There was nothing but a blank wooden wall. There was no sign of Joe and no sign of the Ghost Gunman.

But Heather had seen them both go in, and the only way out was the way Frank had come in.

Where could they be?

Before Frank could consider that more carefully, he had another problem to deal with.

The storm was at its peak now. The water in

70

the boathouse had risen to a point several inches over his head, and a fierce undertow was pulling at Frank's legs.

The undertow dragged him under.

Frank was trapped at the back of the building underwater, and there seemed to be no way out.

Chapter

9

Now the pounding surf was pulling Frank in many directions all at once.

He fought the current, but more important, he also fought the urge to panic. He told himself that he could survive if only he kept his head.

The current was strongest in the center of the building, and Frank reasoned that if he could work his way to a side, he'd have a better chance of escaping. It was the longer route, he knew, but the force of the waves would be less, and he'd have the wall to hang on to.

Strange, he thought as he fought the rising tide, the undertow seemed to be pulling his legs toward the *back* of the building, when it should be pulling in the direction of the doorway and out to sea.

With slow, measured strokes he gradually made his way to the side of the building.

The chilly gray water was laced with salty foam, and Frank had never felt so tired. His clothes were soaked, and the added weight only made his effort harder.

He had no idea how long it had taken, but finally Frank was up against the wall of the building and pulled himself up high enough to keep his head above water.

He was safe, but he wasn't out of the building yet. Frank inched his way to the entrance.

He rested for a minute in the front corner of the building, gathering all his strength to fight his way out.

He tightened his grip on the wall frame and moved through the pounding surf to the open doorway without letting go of the wall. Then he forced his way outside, only to be slammed against the side of the building by an enormous wave.

Treading water, he moved along the outside of the boathouse toward the high ground behind the building.

At last his feet touched firm sand and Frank began to run, slogging as fast as he could up the hill through the rain to the hotel and safety

An hour or so later Frank was sitting in the dining room wearing dry clothes and wrapped in a blanket against the chill. He wondered when he would feel warm again. After all, he was in the tropics.

Police Sergeant Chester Wrenn stood in a corner of the room.

"Any sign of Joe?" Frank asked.

Sergeant Wrenn shook his head no. "But you shouldn't worry too much. I understand your brother is strong and healthy. Chances are good he's somewhere safe waiting for the storm to end."

"I hope you're right," said Frank.

"More tea, Frank?" asked Callie.

"Thanks."

Frank sipped the warm, sweet tea and knew he'd soon recover. He also knew there was so much to be done.

"Has Tyler's body been picked up?" asked Frank.

"Yes," replied Gary. "The sergeant and I got it."

Janet entered the room carrying a tray of sandwiches. "Help yourselves, everyone," she offered.

"Where's Heather?" asked Frank.

"Asleep," Callie told him.

Sergeant Wrenn said, "Now that everybody's here, I'd like to ask a few questions."

"Of course," said Gary, "but this isn't everybody."

Frank nodded as he sipped his tea. As an outsider, he didn't want to come on too strong and was happy that Gary was speaking up.

"Who's not here?" asked Wrenn. He was slender and young and a native islander. He had not acquired the hard edge of an overworked police officer yet.

Janet said, "Two of our guests—Mr. Gaines and Mr. Logan. They're in their rooms, but I'll go get them if you like."

"No," said the sergeant. "I'll speak to them later."

He turned to Frank first and said, "Well, why don't you tell me what you know."

"Right now, what I know is that my brother is out there somewhere," said Frank, gesturing to the storm that continued to rage outside. "And we've got to find him. He may be hurt."

With a patience that seemed genuine, Wrenn said, "We'll do what we can when we can. There's nothing we can do till the storm breaks. I was barely able to get here myself. We can't be risking men's lives."

It was not what Frank wanted to hear. What if Joe was in danger?

"So then," Wrenn continued, "tell me what happened."

With as much detail as he could recall, Frank described the events of the afternoon, starting with the gunshot, finding Tyler's body, dragging it out of the boathouse, and searching for Joe. "Does the boathouse fill up with water often?" Frank asked Gary, interrupting himself.

"Whenever there's a flood tide or a storm. Quite often, really," the young hotel owner answered.

"Is there any reason your brother might have for wanting to shoot Randolph Tyler?" asked the sergeant, returning to the point.

"Of course not!" Callie cried.

"I'm speaking with Mr. Hardy, young lady," said Wrenn. "You'll get your turn."

"My brother would never shoot anyone," Frank said evenly.

"Of course," said Wrenn.

He turned to Gary, Janet, and Callie, who were sitting across from him at the dining room table. "And you, what did you see?"

"Almost nothing," said Janet. "We went out sightseeing and came back when the storm blew up."

"That's right," continued Gary. "When we got here, the storm had hit pretty hard, and we found Heather in the back. She was pretty hysterical by then."

"And what did she say?"

Callie answered. "Very little, at first. She said there'd been a shooting. Call the police. But we couldn't get too much out of her for a while."

76

"I called you," Gary said, "and Janet and Callie put her to bed."

"So then," said the sergeant in his soft, lilting speech, "the situation as I see it is that one of the island's most prominent citizens has been murdered, and there are two possible witnesses: one is hysterical and the other is missing."

He paused and seemed to be enjoying the fact that he was the center of attention. He took a sandwich from the tray, sampled it, and said, "Very good."

He ate in calm silence for a moment and then said, "I will speak with the hysterical young woman." The sergeant nodded at Janet and said, "If you would be so kind as to accompany me to her room?"

"Of course," said Janet.

When they left, Frank shared what he had uncovered at the library with Callie and Gary. He told them about the payments that an official with the initials EBJ had received from Wiley Reed and that the governor in those days was named Elmer Bradley Jamison and that Jamison had disappeared in late 1929.

"Shouldn't you tell all this to Sergeant Wrenn?" asked Callie.

"It's too soon for that," said Frank. "I don't know what any of it means yet, and he's got his hands full just now with the Tyler murder."

Frank turned to Gary and asked, "Does any of

what I told you jibe with what you know about Wiley Reed?''

"As a matter of fact, it does," said Gary, and as the storm howled just outside the dining room window, he regaled Frank and Callie with the highlights of the legend of Wiley Reed and his disappearance.

As Frank listened to Gary he wondered if his brother had vanished into thin air as Wiley Reed had.

Joe was very much alive, and at that very moment was still pursuing the Ghost Gunman

He was no apparition, though. This was a flesh-and-blood man, one who had fought with both Frank and Joe. A man who had probably murdered Randolph Tyler.

They had been playing cat and mouse for hours in a series of tunnels that crisscrossed under all of Runner's Harbor.

The masked gunman, who had bolted past Joe into the darkness of the boathouse, turned almost instantly and sneaked back out the entrance.

He had eluded Joe and ducked into a small shed next to the boathouse.

When Joe got to the shed, it appeared to be empty, but a window on the rear wall had a sill that was three feet thick.

Joe knew no one would construct a window like this, so he poked around until he bumped a small lever on the side of the window, tripping a door. A door leading to a mazelike series of underground tunnels.

After hours of running after the masked man, Joe was totally turned around because all the tunnels were so dark. Airshafts at random intervals offered thin gray shafts of dim light, but generally the corridors were pitch-black.

Spider webs laced across the tunnels and caught on Joe's face and in his hair. Rats screeched and darted at his feet as Joe splashed through puddles of water.

He tried not to think about any of this, but focused all his attention on the gunman. Joe knew he had to stay within earshot of the sound of the man's footsteps and not let him get too far ahead. The darkness and the fact that the killer seemed to have a clear idea of where he was going made things all that much more difficult for Joe.

Wiley Reed was a smart man, thought Joe, and had obviously built this system as a means of avoiding enemies.

It was that confidence in the tunnels that had led to Joe's trying another tracking method. From time to time he would shout at his quarry, "I'll get you! You know I'm going to get you."

The gunman never responded, but the reverberating sound provided Joe with a guide through the darkness.

Joe was getting weary of the chase. It had been

several minutes since he had last heard the killer, and he wondered if the man was still in the tunnels or if he had made an escape. He strained to hear any sign that the gunman was nearby.

Finally his concentration was paying off. He couldn't see the killer, but Joe could hear the man, breathing hard, just a few feet ahead. Joe moved faster.

Once again an airshaft illuminated the passage enough so that Joe could see a turn in the tunnel.

He approached the corner slowly, cautiously, and as quietly as he could.

From around the bend came a whispered plea. "Help me. I'm hurt."

Joe rounded the corner. He had caught his man.

Chapter

10

"Ooomph!" cried Joe as he ran ahead and stumbled over a huge rock in the middle of the tunnel and crashed to the hard floor.

Momentarily dazed, Joe heard the gunman's laughter dead ahead.

The gunman's cries for help had been the bait, and Joe had fallen for it.

In the shadowy recesses of the tunnel, not far from where Joe lay nursing an aching knee, came the unmistakable hissing of a snake. Now Joe was the prey, and the snake was about to attack.

The lingering storm was making Frank very restless, and he knew he had to do something or go crazy.

If he couldn't search for Joe, he could at least search for answers.

Frank was sitting in the dining room with Callie, staring at half a sandwich on his plate. It looked very unappealing to him.

"Is there anything I can get you?" asked Callie.

"No, thanks," answered Frank. "Really. I'm just not hungry."

He was forming a plan of action for the evening when Earl Logan sulked into the dining room and demanded supper. "Where're Gary and Janet?" he growled. "I'm hungry."

"They're in the kitchen," said Callie. "I'll get them for you."

When Gary came out to see what Logan wanted, Frank quietly excused himself, saying he was tired and wanted to lie down. He quickly went to the second floor.

Frank was surprised to find Logan's room unlocked, because the man had been so paranoid every time Frank and Joe had approached him. Frank took it as a sign that his luck was turning for the better in this case.

We could use a little good luck, thought Frank as he forced himself not to think about where Joe might be at that moment.

It was soon clear why Logan felt no need to keep his door locked. There was almost nothing in the room. At least nothing on top of the two chests of drawers.

As quickly as he could, Frank checked out one chest and found only a few pairs of socks and three sets of underwear. In the closet there was nothing. Logan had apparently traveled to Barbados with almost nothing.

The other chest of drawers was completely empty.

There was only one more place Frank could think to search. There he had some luck. Between the mattress and box spring were about a dozen pieces of sheet music. Most of the tunes were old standards, and among them was the Gershwin song "Someone to Watch Over Me."

Of even more interest was a newspaper article from the Sunday magazine section of a 1967 edition of the *Chicago Tribune* that described the adventures of a Prohibition-era bootlegger from Barbados named Wiley Reed. The story told of Wiley's marriage to Millicent and how the song "Someone to Watch Over Me" had been played at their wedding party on the pavilion. The article included a photo of Runner's Harbor and went into great detail about a treasure buried somewhere on the grounds of the hotel that had never been found. It told of the legend of Wiley's ghost and how the ghost now haunted Runner's Harbor, protecting the treasure.

"You need any help rifling through my personal

property, you just let me know," said Earl Logan, standing at the door to his room.

Frank had been sitting on the bed while reading the newspaper account and stood up to face Logan.

"What gives you the right to sneak into my room?" challenged Logan.

"A man's been murdered," said Frank.

"From what I hear, your brother did it."

"My brother's no killer."

"Meaning?"

"Meaning an ex-convict who's playing the piano in the middle of the night to scare people might have a lot of explaining to do."

Logan squirmed a bit in the doorway but said defiantly, "Who says I'm a con?"

"I couldn't help but notice the tattoos on your hands," said Frank. "They're the kind men give one another in prison to pass the time. Do you want me to make a phone call to confirm my suspicion?"

"I did my time. I'm clean."

"I believe you, but tell me about this," said Frank.

Logan's story was simple. He had served more than twenty years for armed robbery, and his last cellmate had been an old-time bootlegger who loved to tell stories about the exploits of the famous Wiley Reed. The old-timer described Runner's Harbor in such detail that Logan felt he had already been there. The most interesting part of the story, which may or may not have been true, was the fact that Wiley's ghost was said to come out at night if "Someone to Watch Over Me" was played on the piano in the pavilion.

"You might say I've had some luck in that regard," said Logan.

The snake hissed again in the darkness, and Joe's instinct was to run, but he knew the snake would attack then, and the snake had the advantage.

What would Frank do? Joe thought. He remembered the incident in Callie's room when Frank had turned on the light to stun the snake, but there were no lights to turn on here. A match wouldn't do the trick.

Joe suddenly realized that the darkness was his friend.

The snake hissed once more, but Joe hoped it would only attack if he made a sudden and quick move.

He pressed his back against the tunnel and inched his way past the boulder the gunman had set in his path. Soon Joe was safely past the snake.

He hurried along now, the pain in his knee reduced to a dull throb. The gunman had been too confident that the trick with the rocks would stop Joe permanently. He could hear the man just ahead, walking slowly, taking his time.

I've got you now, thought Joe.

Soft light glowed ahead as Joe watched the killer open a trap door that led out of the tunnel.

Joe waited until he heard the trap door close and then ran to it. He found the lever to open the door but waited a few seconds before pulling it, hoping that this wasn't a trap.

He did pull the lever finally and hurried up a steep, rough set of stairs and found himself at the back of the house. In the distance he could see the killer running along the water's edge.

The storm had ended and the sun was setting in the western sky.

With renewed confidence Joe resumed his pursuit. The killer's footprints were clear in the wet sand. The killer ran in a straight line toward the pavilion.

Joe slowed down now but kept his quarry in sight. Another figure appeared from the shadows of the pavilion. It was Heather.

Chapter

11

IT COULDN'T BE HEATHER.

Joe stared hard at the pavilion as he ran toward it.

Both the gunman and the person who had met him were no longer in sight. They had ducked into the pavilion.

Joe was torn by conflicting emotions as he ran. Catching the killer would be sweet revenge, but what if Heather was involved?

What could her explanation be? Could it be that the killer forced her into the pavilion? If that was the case then Heather was in danger.

Joe ran faster. When he reached the entrance to the dance pavilion, it was bathed in the lengthening shadows of sunset.

He poked his head inside. The pavilion was empty.

There was no sign of either Heather or the gunman.

Despite his fatigue and the growing darkness, Joe searched for any way the two could have left the pavilion, but he couldn't find one.

There had to be a secret passageway with an entrance to the dance pavilion, and he would uncover it. But not then.

He convinced himself he must have been seeing things when he thought he saw Heather.

Tired, hungry, and confused, Joe walked slowly up the hill to the hotel.

Many lights were glowing in the old building, and he thought he had never seen such a welcome sight. Seeing the hotel conjured up images of dry clothes, food, and sleep that made Joe walk faster.

In the parking lot were several police cars and an ambulance, and Joe found it difficult to believe that he had discovered Randolph Tyler's body only hours earlier. His experiences in the tunnels seemed to have taken days.

Entering the hotel, Joe could hear voices coming from the dining room.

"The storm is over," Frank was saying. "We have to begin searching for my brother now."

"I sympathize with you," said a man whose

voice Joe didn't recognize, "but it is dark now, and I cannot risk the life of anyone else."

Joe stood in the doorway to the dining room unnoticed. He saw Frank and Callie and Gary and Janet and Logan and Gaines, and he also saw several uniformed police officers. The man speaking was a slender, intense islander whom Joe assumed to be a detective.

Joe was disappointed that Heather was not in the room.

Callie saw him first and shrieked, "Joe!" as if she had seen a ghost.

"Joe!" cried Frank, rushing toward his brother.

Frank gave Joe a big hug, and Joe was instantly embarrassed. "What's all the fuss about?"

"We were worried about you," said Frank.

Before Joe could explain what happened, Sergeant Wrenn stepped forward and said, "I'm glad you made it back safely, Mr. Hardy. We have a lot to talk about. Why don't you get cleaned up, get something to eat, and then we can chat."

An hour later Joe, Frank, and Callie were gathered around the dining room table with Sergeant Wrenn.

"How long was I gone, exactly?" asked Joe.

Frank said, "As near as I can estimate, about four and a half hours. The storm hit right around three-thirty, and you showed up here around eight."

Joe shook his head. "It seemed more like four days than four and a half hours."

"Where were you during that time?" asked the sergeant.

Joe said, "Tunnels. Underground. Underneath the hotel—at least I think that's where we were."

"Who is we?" asked Sergeant Wrenn.

Joe glanced at Frank, who nodded a silent yes.

"I don't know who he is, but we've seen him here before. He's the same guy who attacked Frank."

"You were attacked?" said the sergeant.

"It was nothing," said Frank. "Really."

"I think you should let me be the judge of such things. When did this happen?"

"Night before last," said Frank.

"And your assailant got away."

"He vanished into thin air," said Frank. "And that wasn't the first time."

Joe and Frank described the Ghost Gunman and the other incidents.

Sergeant Wrenn paused a moment, formulating his next question. "Please answer this very carefully," he said. "What happened to Randolph Tyler?"

"Well," Joe began, "I had gone to the boathouse to see if I had missed anything that might tie in with the explosion yesterday."

Sergeant Wrenn nodded for Joe to continue.

Joe described how the storm broke just as they

were approaching the boathouse and told them about hearing gunshots over the sounds of the storm.

"You say 'gunshots,'" said Sergeant Wrenn. "How many did you hear exactly?"

"Two."

"Go on."

"After I heard the shots, I took my time going into the boathouse."

"Where was Miss Reed during all of this?" asked the sergeant.

"Excuse me?"

"Miss Reed. Heather Reed. I spoke with her. She is resting at home now."

Joe said, "We spent the day sunbathing, and she went with me to the boathouse."

Sergeant Wrenn's face was expressionless as he said, "What happened after you finally entered the boathouse?"

"Well, I saw Tyler lying there. I wasn't certain at first that he was dead, but he looked bad, and I yelled for Heather to get help."

"What were your exact words?"

Joe thought a moment. "I said, 'Heather, get help. Randolph Tyler's dead. I'm going after the gunman.'"

"Then what?"

Joe described how the gunman had pushed past him and how he had followed the killer out of the boathouse, through the storm, and into the shed. Once again the gunman had vanished.

Sergeant Wrenn said, "And then you found the entrance to the tunnels."

"That's right."

"The tunnels have been talked about on the island for years, of course," said the sergeant, "but to my knowledge, no one has ever actually been in one. I always assumed they were another part of the Wiley Reed myth. He is a genuine cult hero here, as I'm sure you know by now."

Frank and Joe nodded yes.

"And I also assume that neither of you believes this Ghost Gunman, as you call him, is truly a ghost."

Again they agreed. "I hit him on the jaw, and his jaw was real enough," Frank said.

"Curious, though, isn't it? Tell me, then," said the sergeant, "about the tunnels. What happened there? What were they like? How did you find your way out?"

Joe's version of his time underground was complete and had everyone at the table squirming, especially Callie, who still had not fully recovered from her own encounter with a snake.

"And once you were out at the back of the house," asked Sergeant Wrenn, "what did you do?"

Joe said, "I saw him heading for the dance

pavilion and I followed him, but by the time I got there, he was gone.''

"No secret passageway?" asked the sergeant.

"I looked, but couldn't find one. There has to be one, though," said Joe.

Sergeant Wrenn paused for a long time and sipped his coffee in concentrated silence. At last he said, "Very well. I thank you for your cooperation."

"That's it?" asked Joe.

"For now," said the sergeant as he stood up and prepared to leave.

"Am I a suspect?" asked Joe.

"What is that line from your American detective novels?" mused the sergeant. "Ah, yes, 'I suspect nobody and everybody.' "

Frank and Joe sat at the dining room table long after everyone had gone to bed.

Joe told Frank what few details about the tunnel he had forgotten to tell Sergeant Wrenn, and Frank explained what he had discovered in the library, namely that the government official who had been taking bribes from Wiley Reed to cover his rum-running operation was Elmer Bradley Jamison.

"The more I learn about this," said Frank, "the more it seems that our friend Brady Jamison must be involved."

"But we've got no proof," said Joe.

After a short silence Frank said, "I get the feeling you're not telling me everything."

"Why do you say that?" asked Joe.

"Come on, Joe, we're brothers. I know you."

"Nothing, Frank. It's nothing. You're wrong. I'm just tired, that's all."

"It's something to do with Heather, isn't it?" said Frank.

"No," said Joe, a little too forcefully. He repeated the denial in a quieter voice.

"Okay, Joe," said Frank. "Have it your way. But you'd better ask yourself one question before you get in too deep."

"What?"

"What do you really know about Heather?"

Hours later, as he lay in bed, Joe felt truly miserable. He didn't like keeping things from Frank, but he wasn't going to say anything to anyone about Heather until he questioned her himself.

As he lay there, tossing and turning, he considered all the possibilities and kept coming up with different conclusions.

Sometime around three in the morning Joe had had enough. "What's the use hanging around here if you can't sleep," he muttered to himself as he dressed.

He would go to Heather's house and see her immediately. There was no way he was going to get any rest if he didn't. He got dressed and decided to go out the window so no one would hear him leave.

He hung from the window ledge itself for a bit to get his bearings and then reached for a vine to climb down. He had a firm grip around the vine and swung off the ledge when suddenly the vine went slack.

As he fell Joe could see that someone had planted a stake, point up, in the ground just where he would land.

Chapter

12

JOE KEPT FALLING. He thought he'd never land.

He groped in the darkness for something to grab on to, and at the last possible second his right hand caught hold of a clamp that held a drainpipe in place.

His shoulder strained as his full weight hung from the arm that had been wrenched from the jolting stop. He didn't let go, though.

He swung his body toward the building and reached for the pipe with his left hand. Pain seared through his right shoulder as he strained to hold on with one hand.

He was able to get a good grip, and he hung there for a moment, getting his bearings and catching his breath.

What happened? he wondered.

The ground was only ten feet below him, so Joe pushed away from the building in a controlled drop and easily avoided the pointed stake.

He landed with a muffled "Oomph!" Then he stood up and brushed himself off.

There at his feet was the vine. Even in the darkness he could see that it had obviously been cut.

Someone had anticipated that he would use the vine to climb down from his room and had sabotaged him.

But who? Who was behind all these incidents, and why?

"How much do you really know about Heather?" Frank had asked.

As much as I need to know, Joe thought. Or was it enough?

As he walked along the beach to the Tyler Inn, Joe thought about what Heather had told him.

She and her parents, Sam and Betty Reed, had lived for most of her life in one of the cottages at the Tyler Inn, Randolph Tyler's hotel complex just down the beach from Runner's Harbor. Before that she had lived at Runner's Harbor. Apparently her father had managed Runner's Harbor for a time with a partner.

Joe didn't know who that partner was or why the Reeds left Runner's Harbor. After all, Sam Reed was Wiley and Millicent's son. Why did he just work there? How did he lose the place? Or did they still own it?

"What do you really know about Heather?"

Joe knocked softly on the door to cottage number two. Since she had turned eighteen, Heather lived there alone. Her parents lived in number one.

At first there was no answer, but eventually the door was opened by Heather.

He had obviously awakened her. She was wearing a light bathrobe against the night chill and her long hair was tousled.

"Joe?" She was truly surprised. "Joe, you're alive!" She threw her arms around him and hugged him tightly. "I never thought I'd see you again."

"We need to talk," said Joe softly.

Heather took a step back, nodded her head, and said, "Give me a minute," before closing the door.

When she came out, she was dressed in a sweater and jeans and had taken the time to brush her hair. "Walk along the beach?" she said.

At first neither of them spoke. Finally Heather asked, "What's this all about, Joe?"

"I couldn't sleep."

"Some people drink warm milk when that happens."

"I had to talk to you."

"About what?"

"Everything that's been happening around here the last few days," said Joe.

"You mean the murder."

"And the boat explosion."

Heather stopped and looked Joe in the eye. "Ask me anything you want and I'll try to answer."

Joe took a deep breath and said, "Okay. First, where were you all evening?"

"After I ran into your brother and called the police I came here to clean up. I took a bath and fell asleep. You woke me up."

"You've been here the whole time?"

"Yes, Joe. Why?"

He told her what he had seen, or thought he'd seen, at the pavilion.

Heather said, "I know you don't want to hear this, but I've told you before. You saw my grandmother's ghost."

"There are no such things as ghosts, Heather."

"Have it your way. Any other questions?"

Joe thought for a minute. "Yeah, one," he said. "Your father is Wiley Reed's son, right?"

"That's right."

"Then why don't you and your family own Runner's Harbor anymore?"

Heather seemed upset by the question.

"What's wrong?" asked Joe.

"That—that's a touchy subject."

"Why?"

"Well, this all happened when I was a little girl. Obviously we did own Runner's Harbor, but my dad ran into some difficulty managing the place and had to take on a partner."

"Who?"

"Does it matter?"

"It might."

"Well, it was John Jamison."

"Is he any relation to Brady Jamison?"

"He's Brady's father. Why? Is that important?"

"Heather, there's no way of knowing what's important right now." Joe paused a moment, thinking. He asked her, "What happened?"

"You mean how did my folks lose Runner's Harbor?"

Joe nodded.

"Well," said Heather, "it's kind of a long story.

Frank was still asleep when Joe got back to the hotel.

Joe gave the mattress a couple of thumps and said, "Wake up, Frank. It's a beautiful morning and we've got work to do."

It took a few seconds for Frank to clear his head. He stared at his brother as if Joe were insane.

"What's with you?" asked Frank.

"Nothing. Why? I feel great."

Frank forced himself out of bed and began to dress. "Well, it's only eight o'clock, and you're acting kind of strange."

"I've been with Heather."

"This early?" said Frank, startled.

"I couldn't sleep, so I went to her cottage and woke her up, and we walked along the beach and talked. She told me everything, Frank. I mean, I asked her questions and she answered them all. I believe her. I believe she's telling the truth when she says she doesn't know anything about what's been going on."

Frank wasn't convinced, but he sensed that the worst thing he could do just then would be to suggest that to Joe. Instead he said, "That's great, Joe." Frank rubbed his eyes and stifled a yawn. "What did she tell you?"

"Heather says her father had problems keeping Runner's Harbor open, so he got a partner," Joe began.

"Who?"

"John Jamison. Brady's father. Anyway," Joe continued, "Jamison handled the books and didn't pay any taxes. The government closed the place. Heather's parents were innocent of any crime, but they lost Runner's Harbor."

Frank said, "What happened to Jamison?"

"He died in prison."

"I wonder why Tyler didn't buy the hotel

then," wondered Frank. "It must have been available at a tax sale."

"Maybe he didn't have the money," offered Joe.

"Could be," said Frank, lost in thought.

When Frank finished dressing, he and Joe knocked on Callie's door, and then the three of them headed to the dining room for nine o'clock breakfast. On their way they encountered Gary and Janet in the lobby, in a heated discussion with Theresa Farr, who was saying, "This is the last straw."

"But you're not being fair," argued Janet.

"How is it our fault?" demanded Gary.

"Fault, I'm afraid, isn't the issue," said Farr. "Appearances are. A murder was committed here. I have no alternative but to revoke your license."

"We'll fight you in court," said Gary.

"That is your right."

"When will you take our license?" asked Janet in a defeated voice.

"I'll give you two days." With that, Theresa Farr was gone.

"What will you do?" asked Callie.

"We'll fight. We have no choice," said Janet. "Not that it matters much. We're down to our last customer."

"What do you mean?" asked Frank.

"Allistair Gaines checked out this morning," said Gary.

"Where did he go?" asked Joe.

Janet said, "He told me he was checking into the Tyler Inn."

After breakfast Frank and Joe returned to the shed to search for clues. They weren't very deep into the tunnel when Joe spotted a shiny object on the ground.

It was a gold cufflink in the shape of the letter *G*.

"Gaines," said the Hardys in unison.

"We can search in here later," said Frank. "Right now I think you should speak with Mr. Gaines while I check out some more details at the library."

Joe agreed and started down the beach toward the Tyler Inn.

Frank walked slowly to the car he had borrowed from Gary and Janet. Many pieces of the puzzle were beginning to come together for him, but he still had a lot of unanswered questions.

And only two days left to break this case if we're going to save Runner's Harbor for Gary and Janet, he thought as he turned the ignition key.

The sound of the engine was drowned out by the deafening volley of gunfire.

Chapter

13

A BULLET TORE THROUGH the windshield, slid
past Frank's right cheek, and slammed into the
backseat of the car.

The glass from the windshield exploded into
hundreds of tiny rocklike pieces that showered
into his lap.

He ducked under the steering wheel, taking
cover, waiting for another shot to be fired. As he
crouched there he did a mental check and decided
he was okay.

Several seconds passed, and still there was no
more gunfire. The only sound Frank could hear
was the engine idling quietly. Slowly he reached
his hand up and turned the key, and there was
silence.

Frank could hear Callie, Gary, and Janet rush onto the front porch of the hotel.

"Frank?" cried Callie.

"Stay inside!" he shouted.

"Are you okay, Frank?" asked Gary.

"Yes. Just stay there."

More time passed, and Frank took the chance to peer outside the jeep. No one was in sight in any direction. Slowly he eased himself out of the jeep and stood beside it.

He was staring at a nearby palm tree when Callie raced up behind him.

"Frank! Frank!"

She put her arms around him and hugged him tightly. There were tears in her eyes, and she was shaking.

"It's okay," he said quietly, comforting her. "Really. I'm fine."

"Oh, Frank, I thought they really got you this time."

Gary and Janet approached them slowly.

"Are you sure you're okay?" asked Janet.

"I'm fine, really," said Frank.

"What happened?" asked Gary.

"Someone took a shot at me but missed."

Callie said, "This place is really scaring me now."

"That's exactly how someone wants you to feel," said Frank. "And we've got to stop him."

"But how?" asked Janet.

"I think Joe and I are close to the solution," he said. Frank started walking toward the palm tree he'd been studying. "And just so everyone can stop worrying about ghosts, come over here."

He stopped next to the tree and pointed at a metal box taped to the trunk.

"It's just as I thought," he said, pointing at the box.

"What is it?" asked Callie.

"I'll let the police take it down, in case there are any fingerprints on it, but I'm pretty sure it's a small radio device triggered to fire a shot when I turned the key in the ignition of the jeep."

"You can do things like that?" asked Janet.

"Yes," answered Frank.

"What should we do?" asked Gary.

"Call Sergeant Wrenn and tell him what happened. Show him the box. I'm sorry about what happened to your jeep."

"We're just glad you're okay," said Janet.

"Janet's right," said Gary. He stared at his damaged jeep. "I guess you'll need the other car."

"We won't be long," said Frank.

Callie said, "We?"

"If you'd like."

"Definitely," said Callie, giving him another hug. "I think you need someone to watch over you, Frank Hardy."

* * *

Joe Hardy knocked softly on the door to cottage number seven at the Tyler Inn.

"I think he'll be in his room. He seemed to have a lot of unpacking to do," the desk clerk, a portly islander, had said. He also told Joe that Gaines had checked in just two hours earlier.

Number seven was off by itself and did not have an ocean view. Joe suspected it was cheaper than the other rooms and wondered how much money Gaines had.

There was no response to his knock, so Joe rapped harder on the door and said, "Mr. Gaines? It's Joe Hardy. Can I come in?"

From inside he heard feet shuffling, then the door finally flew open. "Welcome, my boy. Welcome," the old man said. "Come in, come in. You're my first visitor in my new home."

Joe entered the small cottage and tried to find a place to sit or even stand. Boxes were stacked in every conceivable place, and most of the stacks reached to the ceiling.

The only things that Gaines seemed to have unpacked were his art supplies. A blank canvas was already resting on an easel in the only vacant corner in the room.

Apparently Joe had arrived just as the old man was about to begin a new painting.

"Sit anywhere," said Gaines as he himself took

the only seat, a small stool that was set up in front of the canvas.

"Thanks," said Joe, standing in place by the door. "I'm fine right here."

"Suit yourself," said Gaines. The old man picked up a brush and began to dip it into the splotches of paint on a nearby palette. It seemed as if Gaines was going to ignore Joe's presence.

"Mind if I ask you a few questions?" asked Joe.

"Of course not, my boy," answered Gaines cheerfully. "I enjoy our little chats." He made a stroke with blue paint on the empty canvas and paused to consider it.

"Why did you check out of Runner's Harbor?" asked Joe.

"That's a fair question. Fair question." Gaines stared at the blue paint.

"And?"

"And what, my boy?"

"What's the answer?"

"Oh, of course, of course. You want answers. I'm being rude." He put down his paintbrush and looked Joe in the eye. "You want to know why I left Runner's Harbor. It's very simple really. Millicent asked me to."

Joe was too stunned to say anything, but Gaines didn't appear to notice Joe's reaction.

"She was very nice about it," Gaines continued. "Said that they needed the rooms and couldn't afford to keep giving me the special rate I had always had. Actually, she found me this room here and was able to work out a special deal with the owners. I'm paying less now than before."

Unsure how to respond to this, Joe simply held out the gold cufflink for Gaines to see.

"My cufflink, thank you. Where did you find it?"

"In the tunnels beneath the hotel."

"How strange," said the old man, fitting the gold *G* into place on his cuff. "That was where I had the conversation with Millicent when she asked me to leave."

"When was that?" asked Joe.

"Oh, two or three weeks ago. She said I could finish out the month and I did."

"You saw Millicent in the tunnels?" asked Joe.

"Yes."

"Millicent. Not Heather," Joe continued.

Gaines paused a few seconds before responding. "May I confess something to you?"

"Of course," said Joe.

"You know that I am the one who painted the portrait of Millicent that hangs in the lobby at Runner's Harbor." Joe nodded his head yes. "Well, my boy, I have been in love with Millicent Reed for more than sixty years. Believe me. It was she."

* * *

Frank and Callie spent most of the day in the library. Frank's research added a few more pieces to the puzzle, but try as she might, Callie couldn't get him to tell her what he had discovered.

"I want to have proof before I tell you or anyone anything," said Frank.

"Even me?" asked Callie.

"Even you."

At the dinner table that evening Callie and the Hardys discovered that Gary and Janet had been busy during the day, too.

Despite the fact that they could lose Runner's Harbor, both of them seemed upbeat and cheerful.

"We decided," said Janet, "that if we had to leave here, we'd at least leave with a bang."

"So we're having a party tonight," said Gary.

"A party?" asked Callie.

"Yes," said Janet. "A big dance in the pavilion."

"And we invited everyone in town," Gary said.

By eight o'clock that night it seemed that everybody on the island had accepted the invitation.

The pavilion was cool as a mild breeze blew in off the ocean. The decorations that Janet and Callie had hung swayed gently in the wind. They had arranged several tables around the edges of the floor and placed trays of food and bowls of punch on each one. Gary and Janet were running around, making sure that everyone had a good time.

The guests, meanwhile, were milling about idly.

"Why isn't anyone dancing?" Callie asked Joe and Frank.

Frank looked at her with a curious grin on his face. "There's no music."

As if on cue, Earl Logan walked to the piano and sat down. He calmly took out a batch of sheet music, chose one, and began to play.

"Frank," said Callie, "it's the same song we heard our first night here. 'Someone to Watch Over Me.' "

"Is it?" asked Frank.

"You know it is, don't you?"

"I know many things," teased Frank.

"Did you ask Logan to play it?"

"You ask too many questions. Would you like to dance?"

"What's going on here, Frank Hardy?"

"I'm on vacation and I'm at a party and I'd like to dance with the prettiest girl here."

"Flattery will get you everywhere," said Callie as Frank led her to the dance floor.

Meanwhile, Joe saw Heather walk onto the dance floor. She seemed distracted, as if something was wrong. Joe approached her. She smiled when she saw him and immediately said yes when he asked her to dance.

"Everything okay?" asked Joe.

"It is now," Heather whispered.

After a few slow circles Joe stopped dancing and pulled away from Heather. "Do you hear it?" he asked.

"What?" she replied.

"Someone's screaming."

The warning cries seemed unreal at first. They seemed especially out of place at a friendly dance on a warm night in an outdoor pavilion overlooking the ocean.

But there they were. "Fire!" someone was shouting.

"Fire!" screamed another person, and then the whole crowd took up the cry.

One whole corner of Runner's Harbor was engulfed in flames.

Chapter

14

THE MUSIC STOPPED, and the crowd ran toward the hotel.

"Come on, Joe!" shouted Frank. "Let's go!"

The Hardys ran in the direction of the fire, and most people followed them.

Bright orange waves of flame billowed out from a second-story window.

Frank saw Gary standing by the building, staring anxiously at the blaze. Gary said, "I called the fire department. They should be here in a few minutes."

"Good," said Frank. "If we can just contain it, we should be okay. Is anyone inside?"

"No. I checked."

Frank turned to the people who had gathered

nearby. They all stood still, watching Runner's Harbor burn.

"We need your help till the fire department gets here," Frank told them. "Divide yourselves into smaller groups and find buckets and hoses. Let's try to contain this fire if we can't put it out."

The people in the crowd began to mumble to one another. In a few moments they began to take action, and Frank said, "Joe, Gary, show them where to find things and what to do."

"Right," said Gary, and he motioned to a group of six men to follow him to get tools to fight the fire.

Joe said, "Come with me," to another group of men. He led them around the side of the hotel to a garden hose, and they started spraying the fire with water.

In just a few minutes the dance crowd had been organized into a fairly efficient fire-fighting team, and Frank, who was working next to Gary, felt more hopeful that they would save most of the hotel.

"Any idea how it started?" asked Frank.

"No," said Gary. "I was in the kitchen getting more food when I smelled gasoline."

"Gasoline?" said Frank.

Gary nodded. "Then I heard a sort of whooshing sound. I called the fire department, then I started upstairs. I got to the landing, saw flames, and came back down."

"Is there any chance it could have started by accident?" asked Frank.

"A chance, I suppose, but somehow I doubt it. Somebody just doesn't want us here," said Gary. "And it looks like they're going to get their way."

Joe appeared from the darkness. His face was bright red from working so close to the flames. His red cheeks were smudged with soot and dripping with sweat. "I think we're winning," he said.

Before Frank and Gary could respond, there was a noise in the shadows.

At that moment the Ghost Gunman dashed from the hotel, waving a pistol. He paused in the doorway, his black figure a silhouette against the flames.

He fired a single shot in the air and then raced into the darkness in the direction of the beach.

Earl Logan shouted, "It's Wiley! Stop him!" and he ran off after the mysterious figure.

Without saying a word, Joe gave chase.

"No, Joe!" cried Frank. "Stay and help with the fire."

It was too late. If Joe heard his brother, he gave no sign of it, and soon all three of the running figures were gone.

"What should we do?" asked Gary.

"We have to contain this fire," said Frank.
"It's not over yet."

"But what about Joe?"

"He can take care of himself."

Joe took off through the darkness behind a ghost runner.

The light from the blazing fire behind him cast long flickering shadows on the ground that stretched across the sand and disappeared into the churning black surf, which was an aftermath of the storm the day before.

Logan was just a dim shape in the distance, and he had a big lead on Joe despite the fact that he was much older.

Joe told himself he had to catch Logan because, somehow, Logan was a key to the Ghost Gunman.

For several seconds he lost sight of the older man, but he knew Logan had been heading for the boathouse.

Joe stumbled over a huge piece of driftwood as he heard a voice in the darkness that reassured him and made him feel uneasy at the same time.

"I'll find you, Wiley!" Logan screamed into the night. "You can't escape again!"

Logan was near the boathouse.

Joe ran on toward the sound.

He found Logan on the long wooden dock that jutted out from the boathouse into the water.

Although he was alone, the older man was still shouting at the top of his lungs.

"Not fair! Not fair! Not fair!"

Joe approached him cautiously.

"What's not fair?" Joe asked quietly.

Logan did not hear him at first and continued to rail in the night.

"Not fair! Not fair! All those years, it isn't fair!"

Joe spoke louder this time. "What isn't fair?"

Logan stopped and stared at Joe as if he'd never seen him before. "Wiley, of course."

Joe walked slowly along the rickety dock toward Logan, who was leaning on the railing on the ocean side of the old wooden structure. Joe said, "What about Wiley isn't fair? Wiley's dead."

"No!" screamed Logan. "He's alive. Didn't you see him?"

"I saw someone, but how do you know it was Wiley?"

"It had to be him!"

"But why?"

Before Logan could answer, the turbulent water made the dock tremble violently beneath them so that both men were knocked off their feet.

Struggling to stand up, Joe said, "Let's go someplace and talk about this."

"No. He'll get away. He always gets away!"

The storm the day before had apparently severely damaged the old dock, and Joe was afraid it wasn't going to hold up much longer. He knew Logan was in no condition to be reasoned with. He said, "What brought you to Runner's Harbor?"

"The jewels," said Logan.

The dock shook again, and both men grabbed hold of the railing to steady themselves. This time the simple act of holding the rail seemed to calm Logan. He collected his thoughts and said, "You spend twenty years in prison, you hear all kinds of stories, but this one—"

"Why were you in prison?"

"Does it matter?"

"Does it?" asked Joe.

"Do you mean, was I guilty?"

Joe nodded.

Logan said, "I did twenty years in Joliet for robbing a bank, and yes, I was guilty." He seemed proud, not that he had robbed a bank but that he had the honesty to admit it. "And I don't think a day went by in those twenty years that I didn't hear about the great Wiley Reed."

"From whom?" asked Joe.

"My cellmate," said Logan.

"Who was that?"

But Logan seemed not to have heard the question. He was lost in his memories.

Whoever Logan's cellmate had been, he had filled Logan with stories about the great Wiley

Reed. In particular, about the cache of jewels that Wiley supposedly had with him the night of his last run. The night he vanished.

"It's all over for me now," said Logan.

"What do you mean, 'It's over'?" asked Joe.

Logan stared at him as if Joe were the one who was crazy.

"It's over. I'm tapped out. Broke. Busted. I haven't got a cent to my name. Tonight was it. I was gonna find that treasure and be on easy street, but instead, he got away again, and I'll never find the treasure. They said he always got away, and he's done it again. You saw him. What could I do?"

"Nothing," said Joe, trying to make sense of everything he was hearing.

"Nothing is right."

"Tonight," said Joe.

"Uh-huh."

"You played the piano tonight."

"Learned in the pen. Practiced that song for twenty years."

"And you played it in the middle of the night when we first got here," said Joe.

"I played it a lot," said Logan. "I had to try everything to lure Wiley out of hiding."

"Why give up now?"

"Told you. Got no money. The treasure was my only hope."

"There's always hope. You can find work."

"Who's going to hire a fifty-year-old ex-con?"

"A lot of people," said Joe, noticing that the dock was beginning to sway beneath them.

"You could play the piano sometime. Here at the hotel, maybe."

"Maybe," said Logan, considering the idea. He didn't look too convinced, though.

The tide was rolling in now with full force, and the combination of the damage done by the storm and the weight of the two men was taking its toll on the old dock. It began to lurch violently. Joe struggled to hang on.

Without warning the part of the dock that Logan was standing on collapsed, and with a muffled cry Logan was washed away by the fierce current of the tide.

"Reach for my hand!" cried Joe, lying down flat and desperately reaching out with his hand toward where Logan had just been. It was too late. Logan was gone.

The dock began to crumble under Joe's feet, and he was certain that he, too, would be sucked out to sea. He grabbed for something to hold on to, found a short section of railing, and held on as tightly as he could.

At that moment the small section of dock that he was on broke loose, and he dropped into the water and would have been lost if it hadn't been for the grip he had on that railing.

It wasn't the railing that gave way. It was still securely anchored, and it wasn't a railing.

It was a lever.

Joe's weight was forcing it into a position it hadn't been in for sixty years.

Joe looked up and watched as the rear wall of the boathouse was swung to one side and the entrance to a secret cove opened up in the hill behind it.

Logan really had found it, but he would never know.

As suddenly as the old machinery had been brought back to life after so many years, it collapsed into a dusty heap of wood.

Behind it was a cavern large enough to hide a boat from the curious eyes of U.S. inspectors on the lookout for shipments of rum.

Joe pulled on the lever and raised himself out of the water and onto the remaining section of solid dock. He crawled off the dock into the boathouse and walked cautiously into a place that no one had entered for sixty years.

Chapter

15

IT TOOK THE FIRE DEPARTMENT well into the
night to finally bring the blaze under control.

All during the effort, Frank worried about Joe.
Where could he be? Was he back in the tunnels
underground? Was he in pursuit of the Ghost
Gunman? Was the Ghost Gunman after him?
What, if anything, did Earl Logan have to do with
all of this?

Frank had also given a lot of thought to who
could have set Runner's Harbor ablaze. The fire
had convinced him more than ever that he knew
who was behind all of this.

But it was only a hunch.

He knew he would need solid evidence to take
to Sergeant Wrenn. He had to be able to prove

his case to force them to let Gary and Janet keep Runner's Harbor open.

He had to prove it soon, because it was well past midnight and time was running out.

Finally the last embers of the fire were sizzling and dying as a final spray of water washed over them.

Only a handful of people remained. Once the fire department had arrived, most everyone left.

Now the diehards were finally saying good night to Gary and Janet, thanking them for everything.

When everyone had left, Janet gave Gary a big hug, but they said nothing.

Frank could guess what they were thinking. There weren't going to be any other dances. Gary and Janet were about to lose Runner's Harbor. Once more Frank vowed not to let that happen.

Callie walked up to him and gave him a hug. She looked exhausted after helping to put out the fire.

"How're you doing?" asked Frank.

"Tired," said Callie. "How about you?"

"I'll be okay."

"You two amaze me," said Frank to Gary and Janet, who were standing arm in arm, smiling.

"Why?" asked Janet.

"Well, you've just spent the night trying to save the hotel you may not own by the end of the day tomorrow, and you're smiling."

"What else can we do?" asked Gary.

"Gary's right," said Janet. "We met a lot of nice people tonight. We did save the hotel. And tomorrow's another day."

"Right," said Gary.

"I'm beat," said Callie.

Janet said, "I think we could all use a good night's sleep."

Frank said, "I'm not sure I can sleep until I know where Joe is."

The four of them walked back into the hotel.

As they walked, Frank said, "You know, I was thinking. If the fire had been set in one of the sections that was already renovated, which has sprinklers, this fire would have been a lot easier to fight."

"You're right," said Gary with a yawn.

"Is that important?" asked Callie. "I mean, as far as solving this case goes?"

"It could be," said Frank. "It may mean that whoever set the fire knew a lot about the hotel. Of course, if Tyler hadn't dragged his feet on the construction, the whole place would have had a sprinkler system by now."

"Well, it wasn't so much Tyler's fault as it was Brady Jamison's," said Janet.

"What are you saying?" asked Frank.

"Just that," answered Janet.

Gary said, "Janet's right. Tyler didn't seem to care one way or another, but Brady seemed to make it a special mission to check and recheck every detail.''

"Yes," said Janet as the four of them paused at the bottom of the lobby stairs. "Brady said he wanted everything to be perfect, but it sure seemed to me that he was stalling.''

Callie yawned and stretched, then said, "You people can all talk the night away, but I'm going to bed.''

She kissed Frank good night on the cheek.

Gary and Janet said good night and headed for their room.

Frank stayed where he was. He seemed very distracted.

"Aren't you going to bed, Frank?" asked Callie.

"No. I couldn't sleep with Joe out there. He may be in trouble. I'm going out to look for him.''

Joe Hardy entered the hidden cavern and told himself that no one had probably entered it in more than sixty years.

Or left it, he thought.

He carefully stepped over large sections of the wall of the boathouse that had hidden this secret place for so long.

This must have been Wiley Reed's hideaway, Joe thought. He couldn't see much in the darkness but moved as best as he could by his sense of sound. He was walking on a wooden dock that seemed to circle the water.

Somewhere, not too far ahead of him, he could hear what sounded like a boat rocking in the water. The collapse of the dock outside and the entrance to the wharf had certainly stirred up the water, and as he walked, Joe heard the unmistakable sound of waves lapping against wood.

Eager to see what was there, Joe searched his pockets and found a wet pack of paper matches.

It was his only hope.

He struck one on the package. Nothing. He tried another one. It was wet, too.

The third match did catch fire, and Joe held it out in front of him to get his first glimpse of the boat.

It was resting some thirty feet away, tied to a piling and rocking gently back and forth in the water.

About five feet from him Joe saw a torch sitting in a rack mounted on the wall. He lit the torch with the last bit of flame from the match. It took a few seconds, but soon the torch was blazing brightly, and Joe could proceed.

The boat was about thirty feet long. As Joe moved closer he could see its name painted on the bow.

It was the *Reed Runner*.

Joe had found Wiley Reed's lost boat.

He wanted to feel good about his discovery,

but the cavern was so desolate and spooky that Joe couldn't feel good about anything right then.

Still, he knew what he had to do.

He had to board the boat. This mystery had to be solved once and for all.

Joe paused at the edge of the boat to get his balance. The old motorboat was still rocking awkwardly in the rough water.

Joe had his left hand on the ship's rail while his right hand clutched the torch. His right foot was balancing on the dock as he eased his left foot over the rail and then jumped aboard.

For the first time in more than sixty years the *Reed Runner* had a new passenger.

Joe stood there a moment, getting his sea legs and trying to figure out what to do.

The deck seemed empty, and he decided the logical place to check first would be the wheelhouse.

Slowly he walked along the rocking deck. He had one hand on the rail and the other on his torch.

The bridge was just ahead.

The boat lurched in the water, and Joe lost his balance, waving the torch awkwardly in the direction of the wheelhouse. The flame cast an eerie light, but he had no difficulty picking out the figure at the wheel of the ship.

It was the remains of a man. Bits and pieces of

rotting clothing clung here and there to the slender bones of the skeleton.

Joe stared in amazement at the sight. He tried to stay calm and regain his balance in the tiny space.

When the boat finally stopped rocking, he held the torch overhead to cast a clear light on the scene. The flame made the right hand of the skeleton burn red as it cradled a large and priceless ruby.

He recognized it immediately as the ruby pendant Millicent Reed wore in the painting that hung in the hotel lobby.

Joe was certain he had found Wiley Reed. He told himself that there was no further reason for him to hang around any longer. He would take the ruby and go for help. Joe didn't like the idea of pulling the gem from the skeleton's grasp, but it had to be done. With a quick tug he removed it.

Joe shoved the ruby into one of the pockets of his jeans and moved quickly out of the wheelhouse and toward the dock. As he raised a leg to vault across the rail onto the dock, a shot rang out. A bullet just missed Joe's ear.

He wasn't about to give a second bullet a chance, so he dived off the boat and onto the dock. He landed hard but rolled over quickly to his feet, nearly singeing himself with the torch, and began to run.

He was running away from the entrance. Where should he go? What should he do with the torch? If he kept it, he was a clear target. If he dropped it, he was lost.

The answer came just then. A set of stairs that wound off to the right loomed just ahead, and Joe memorized its location. He threw the torch far out into the water, where it died with a sharp hiss. Then there was complete darkness.

As he felt his way up the winding stone stairs, it occurred to Joe that there had been only one shot.

Was he still being followed?

Never mind, he told himself. You've got the ruby, and these stairs may lead to safety.

The staircase went on for what seemed forever, and when Joe stepped on the next-to-last step, a door at the top of the steps began to open with a whirring sound. Joe took a deep breath and stepped up through an opening in the floor.

The gunshot came from the direction of the boathouse, but when Frank got there he found, instead of the boathouse, a gaping entrance to a cavern. He had a penlight in his pocket and hurried through the musty cave.

"Joe? Are you in here?" he cried, but the only answer was his echo.

Frank was amazed as he noticed the *Reed*

Runner, but passed up examining it for the stairs his penlight had just illuminated.

Halfway up the stairs he guessed that they would end up in the pavilion.

Near the top he heard vioces.

Frank peeked out the trap door. He was right— it was the pavilion. Joe was standing about fifteen feet away with his hands in the air, a ruby necklace dangling in his left hand.

Across the large room was the Ghost Gunman. In his right hand was a pistol, and it was pointed right at Joe.

Chapter

16

JOE WAS SILENT, waiting for the killer to make a move.

Frank stayed hidden in the secret entrance to the wharf, planning a course of action.

"I'll take that," said the gunman, motioning at the ruby.

There was something familiar about the voice, but Frank could not quite place it.

Joe handed over the ruby but still said nothing.

The Ghost Gunman put the ruby in a pocket and said, "Surprised to see me, aren't you?"

Joe said, "A little. It was you shooting at me, wasn't it?"

"I'm a ghost," said the gunman with a laugh. "I can be many places at once."

"Funny," said Joe. "I never believed in ghosts."

"Believe in this, then," snarled the killer, waving his pistol at Joe again. "Where are the rest of the jewels?"

"That was all I found," said Joe.

"Liar! Millicent Reed had tons of jewels. Everyone knows that. Just look at her portrait. And Wiley and the jewels were never found until you stumbled on them tonight. Where are they?"

"I'm telling you the truth, that's all I found."

"I should have killed you before when I had the chance," the gunman said in disgust.

"What do you mean?" As he spoke, Joe began slowly to circle the gunman, looking for a weak spot and a time to attack.

"It would have been so easy, too," the gunman continued. "Right after I set the fire, I saw you and your brother running around, taking charge, acting like you owned the place. I almost did it then."

"Did what?" said Joe, inching nearer to the killer.

"Put a bullet in your brain, what do you think?"

"Why didn't you?" asked Joe.

Standing in the darkness, Frank thought, good move, Joe. Keep him talking.

"You talk tough now, don't you?" said the

gunman. "But you wait. Just wait. And stand still."

"I'm not so tough," Joe protested. "I'm just curious."

"Oh, I was going to shoot you, even with a crowd around, but that fool Logan started chasing me."

Frank found it almost impossible to believe that Logan's interference had saved Joe's life.

"Then what happened?" asked Joe, moving a little closer to the gunman.

"Do you think I can't tell that you're trying to sneak up on me? Do you think I'm stupid?" He waved the gun threateningly at Joe.

"No," said Joe, taking a step backward.

The gunman said, "I'm only talking to you because eventually I'm going to kill you. Now, where are the rest of the jewels?"

"Maybe I know and maybe I don't," said Joe.

A smile formed beneath the black mask. "Now, at least, we're getting somewhere."

"Of course," said Joe, "there's a chance they don't exist at all. Maybe Gaines just invented them for his painting."

"Doubtful. That senile old artist couldn't invent something like that."

Frank thought, Gaines wasn't senile sixty years ago when he painted the portrait of Millicent Reed.

"You said you had other chances to kill me," said Joe. "What happened to you then?"

"I got away from Logan, and then I heard you running after him," the gunman began. "I couldn't believe my luck. Here you were, running right into my trap."

"You didn't go into the tunnels as I expected," said Joe.

"I'm telling you, I'm not stupid. That was the first place you would have looked. I was waiting outside the boathouse. If you'd gone in there, you would be dead."

"You heard my conversation with Logan," guessed Joe.

"The whole boring thing. I was ready to shoot you when you lucked into the wharf."

The gunman dropped his gun hand for just a second and said, "I've been looking for that ship for years, and you found it by accident. By accident!"

"Now, Joe!" shouted Frank.

Startled, the gunman turned in the direction of Frank's voice, and in that split second Joe was on top of the killer.

Despite the size advantage that Joe had over the gunman, the smaller man put up a good fight.

Joe grabbed hold of his wrist and tried to wrestle the gun loose, but the killer would not let go.

The two men toppled to the floor in a rolling struggle. Joe forced himself up on one knee, freed his right hand, and swung at the gunman but missed.

Frank stepped in and wrenched the pistol from the killer's hand.

"Don't move," said Frank.

Joe stood up, but the gunman lay on the floor. "Thanks, Frank," said Joe.

"It's what brothers are for."

"Now, my friend," said Joe to the gunman, "I think it's time we saw your face."

He reached down and began slowly to pull up the black cloth that hid the identity of Randolph Tyler's murderer.

A woman's voice said, "Don't do that, Joe."

Joe and Frank both turned in response.

"Drop the gun," said Heather, who stood some twenty feet away. She was holding an automatic pistol and had it aimed at Joe.

"I mean it, Joe," she said, her voice almost a whisper. "Drop the gun, Frank."

Frank let the pistol fall to the floor.

The gunman grabbed it quickly and stood up and walked toward Heather. "What took you so long?" he demanded of her. "They could have killed me."

Heather didn't answer him. She just kept her automatic leveled at Joe and Frank. Finally she whispered to the killer, "Go on. Get out of here."

"You coming, too?" he asked.

She nodded. "I'll be right behind you."

Joe stared at Heather, not believing what he heard.

The gunman ran from the pavilion and disappeared into the darkness.

Heather began walking backward slowly in the direction the gunman had gone. Joe stood still, watching her, his mouth agape. There was a confused expression on his face.

Heather seemed on the verge of tears. "I'm sorry, Joe. Really," she said.

Joe took a step forward.

"Stop right there," said Heather in a stronger voice. She held the pistol with both hands now.

"But, Heather, why?" asked Joe.

"I had to."

"I don't get it. I thought we were—" Joe didn't finish the thought.

"We are," she said. "Or at least, we were," she added quietly.

Joe took another step toward her and said, "But—"

Heather changed her expression. "Don't come any closer, Joe," she said. "I mean it. I'll shoot."

Frank held out an arm to stop his brother. "She means it, Joe."

With that, Heather turned and ran after the Ghost Gunman.

The Hardys stood in stunned silence for a few seconds. Joe couldn't believe what had just happened. Frank had half expected it and was now planning their next move.

"I know you're not ready to hear this, Joe," he said, "but we've got to stop them, and I don't think we have much time."

Joe said nothing but continued to stare at the place where Heather had been standing. He was still trying to digest what had taken place.

"Joe? Do you hear me?"

Still Joe said nothing.

"Joe, for Gary and Janet's sake, we have to act now. That gunman character is a killer, and if I'm not mistaken, he has an escape planned, and we don't have a moment to spare."

Joe Hardy turned to look at his brother and said, "Let's get him." His look was determined.

Frank Hardy smiled and gave his brother a look that said he knew he could always count on him, no matter what.

"This way," said Frank, and he let Joe back down the secret stairs to the cavern.

"There's no way the gunman will leave without checking for the other jewels on Wiley Reed's boat one more time," Frank said quietly as they walked down the stairs.

The stairs were dark, but Frank still had his penlight, and using it sparingly, the Hardys were able to navigate the dark stairs fairly quickly.

Joe was about to say something, but Frank gestured for him to keep silent.

Ahead of them, coming from the direction of Wiley Reed's boat, they could now hear the sound of people arguing.

It was Heather and the Ghost Gunman.

As they listened to the argument, the Hardys made their way toward the boat.

"I don't understand what you're saying," pleaded Heather. "We had a deal."

"The same deal your grandfather gave mine, right?" snapped the gunman. "Look at this. Don't you see what it means?"

"No," sobbed Heather, sounding afraid.

The Hardys rounded the corner at the bottom of the stairs and sneaked a look out at the boat. There, in the light of the glowing torch, stood the gunman and Heather.

They were about fifty feet away from the boat, and each of them was still holding a gun.

The gunman was hovering over another skeleton, a second one, that was in a crouched position clutching a gun.

"It's only fair," said the gunman.

"What?" asked Heather.

"That I get to keep all the jewels."

"Why?"

"It's obvious that Wiley could never have operated without my grandfather's help, and Wiley betrayed him."

"I don't see it that way," said Heather, now raising her automatic at the gunman.

"What you see doesn't concern me anymore," said the gunman, and he slowly raised the black mask to reveal his face.

It was Brady Jamison.

"We had a deal!" cried Heather.

"Look at him," said Brady, pointing at the remains of his grandfather. "Wiley Reed did that."

He knelt beside the skeleton and lifted the gun from its bony grasp.

"This debt has to be paid!" cried Brady as he threw the old gun at Heather.

Catching her off guard, he swung his gun in her direction. Laughing, he pulled the trigger at point-blank range.

Chapter

17

THE BULLET GRAZED HEATHER on the arm, and she screamed and fell to the ground.

Joe yelled an angry "No!" and charged straight at Brady, tackling him just as he squeezed off another bullet. The impact of Joe's charge caused the bullet to fly harmlessly up in the air, and the gun flew out of Brady's hand as he and Joe tumbled to the ground.

Frank ran to retrieve the gun.

Once again Brady would not surrender easily.

He landed a quick jab to Joe's throat that stunned Joe momentarily, but adrenaline revived him almost instantly.

He used his weight and strength to roll Brady over onto his back, and then Joe knocked the man out with a single blow.

Joe slowly got to his feet and stood over Jamison. He stared at the killer for several seconds and then walked away in disgust.

With gun in hand Frank helped Jamison to his feet and began to lead him back off the wharf toward the stairs.

Joe approached Heather slowly.

No matter what she had done, he still had feelings and cared for her.

She lay on the ground, crying softly to herself. The wound in her arm was not serious. Luckily for her, Brady Jamison was not such a great shot.

Still Joe said, "Are you okay?"

She looked up at him, tears in her eyes, and nodded her head yes.

"Why?" Joe asked, shaking his head.

Heather studied him for a long time and then said, "I'm not sure anymore."

The next morning Joe was the last one down to the dining room for breakfast.

Frank was sitting next to Callie on one side of the big table, and across from them were Gary and Janet.

Joe was surprised to see that Sergeant Wrenn was also there.

"Morning," said Joe as he walked to the sideboard to pour himself a glass of orange juice.

"Good morning," they said in unison.

Janet got up from her chair and said, "Can I get you some eggs and bacon?"

"Yes, please," said Joe, and Janet smiled and headed for the kitchen.

Frank said, "Well, now that Joe's here, we can get started answering Sergeant Wrenn's questions."

"That would be helpful," said Sergeant Wrenn.

He took a sip of coffee and put down his cup. He reached into a shirt pocket and took out a small notebook and pen. "I'm not exactly certain where we should begin," he said. "I hope you can clarify the many confusions I have."

"We'll try," said Frank.

Sergeant Wrenn began, "Well, I guess we should start with what we know. Brady Jamison was the person posing as the ghost running around Runner's Harbor."

"Yes," said Callie, "but I'm not sure why."

"Yeah," said Gary. "All along we thought Randolph Tyler was behind our problems. Say, why didn't he buy the hotel two years ago when we did?"

"Actually," said Frank, "he just didn't have the money. The hotel itself had less to do with what was happening than we all thought."

"I do hope you can explain these things," said the detective, "because I'm afraid young Mr. Jamison isn't doing any talking."

"And Heather?" asked Callie.

The sergeant said, "We have placed her in the hospital as a precaution for her wound, though it is quite superficial. She may be willing to talk eventually, but I'm not so sure she knows all that much."

"I suspect she knows very little," said Frank. He looked at his brother and hoped this bit of news would make things a little easier for Joe.

Gary said, "Well, then, Frank, why is it you think the hotel didn't have so much to do with all of this? After all, Brady Jamison was pretending to be a ghost, and that hurt business."

"The ghost routine was his cover so that he could snoop around the tunnels and hidden passageways more easily," Frank explained. "If people saw him, as they occasionally did, he wouldn't run the risk of being recognized."

"That makes sense," said Janet, who had returned from the kitchen with a plate of food for Joe.

"That was Brady's main goal. He wanted the jewels. I suspect that if he'd found them sooner, he'd have left here and your troubles would have ended."

Callie looked puzzled. "How do you explain the snake in my bedroom that first night?"

"My guess is that it happened one of two ways," said Frank. "It might have been an accident. Brady's snooping around roused the snake in the tunnels, and it could have crawled up into the room, or more likely, he did put it there to scare us away."

"Well, it worked on me." Callie laughed a bit nervously.

"And the piano playing?" asked Gary.

It was Joe's turn to answer. "That was Logan," he said. "Although I have to admit, I'm not quite sure what he hoped to accomplish."

"Yes," said Sergeant Wrenn, looking up from his notebook. "That part has puzzled me also."

Frank smiled. "You have to remember that Earl Logan completely accepted the legend of Wiley Reed and believed to his dying moment that it was Wiley's ghost that was haunting Runner's Harbor."

"But why play the piano? That doesn't seem to make any sense," said Janet.

"It does, or did, to him," said Frank. "Logan spent nearly half his life in prison just thinking about the legend of Wiley Reed and all those jewels. He was obsessed with the idea of finding the gems and being rich. He played the piano in hopes of luring Wiley's ghost out into the open. He thought the ghost would then lead him to the treasure."

"That's sad," said Callie.

The people at the table were silent for a moment.

Gary said, "But how did Logan learn about Wiley and the hotel and the jewels?"

Joe said, "He said his cellmate hardly talked about anything else."

"Did he say who that was?" asked the sergeant.

"No," said Joe. "He died before he answered me."

Frank said, "Well, we can verify it later, but I'm almost certain his cellmate had to be John Jamison."

"Brady's father," said Callie.

Frank nodded.

The sergeant asked, "How did Wiley get his boat in and out of the secret cave if the only entrance was through the boathouse?"

"I'll take this one," said Frank. "It had us confused until we remembered the night of the storm and the boathouse flooding with water. Wiley couldn't take the boat in or out—except on a flood tide. He'd have to plan his trips around the tides, but it obviously worked."

It was Joe's turn to look puzzled now. "Wait a minute," he said. "Was Logan responsible for the song I heard in my room the second night?"

"No," said Frank. "That was Brady again."

"But how?" asked Callie.

Frank pulled a tiny tape recorder out of his pants pocket and set it on the table. He pressed the Play button and "Someone to Watch Over Me" began to play. "I found this in the tunnels the other night. Brady made the mistake of leaving his initials on it. He planted it in a convenient place and turned it on.''

''But why?'' asked Joe.

''So that you would see Heather and think she was Millicent,'' said Callie.

''Exactly,'' said Frank.

''One thing I don't get,'' said Callie. ''If Heather and Brady were in on this together, who planted the bomb in Heather's boat?''

''It is a good question,'' said Sergeant Wrenn. ''Do you have the answer for that one?''

''Actually,'' Frank began, ''though I can't prove this, I'm certain that Heather and Brady planted it there themselves.''

''To divert suspicion away from Heather,'' said Joe.

''Right,'' said Frank. ''My theory is that they were worried that people were going to suspect that there was no ghost of Millicent Reed, that it was Heather all along, and they needed to make Heather appear to be a victim.''

''But Heather could have drowned,'' said Callie. ''Joe saved her life.''

''Or Heather could have pretended to be drowning,'' said Frank. ''Remember, she is an expert sailor.''

''But murder,'' said Janet. ''I mean, it's one thing to harbor a grudge and to search for missing jewels, but to kill a man—''

Frank said, ''Brady and his family blamed the

Tylers and the Reeds for every bad thing that happened to them for many generations. I think Tyler unknowingly crossed Brady one time too many, and Brady just shot him. We're not dealing with a rational man here.''

"And the radio-controlled gunshot from the tree that almost killed you, Frank?" asked Gary. "That was Brady, too?"

"I can answer that one," said the detective. "My men were able to trace the mechanism to a small shop in the city, and the owner has already identified Mr. Jamison as the purchaser. No matter what happens in the Tyler case, we'll be able to convict him of the attempted murder of Mr. Hardy.''

Janet said, "So all of this goes back sixty years or more. I'm confused about one point. If Brady could disappear from the pavilion, he must have escaped down a secret staircase. But he never knew about the cavern until last night, so he didn't go down those stairs. Is there another set of stairs from the pavilion to the tunnels?"

"You're right," said Frank. "There are two trap doors in the pavilion—one leading to the tunnels, the other to the cavern. When he found the one to the tunnels, he probably didn't look farther. He just assumed there'd be only one.'' He reached into his pocket then and pulled out a small leather pouch. "I almost forgot the best part.''

"What's that?" asked Callie.

"I went back to Wiley's boat early this morning, snooped around, and found this in a small chest."

Frank poured the contents of the pouch onto the table. It was the jewels from the portrait on the landing and others besides.

"Millicent's diamonds!" exclaimed Janet.

"Yes, and I believe they belong to you and Gary," said Frank. He turned to the detective. "Am I right?"

"Yes. They own the property."

Frank said, "Now you can afford to fix up the hotel."

"But we've lost our license," said Gary, suddenly changing his expression.

"Actually," said Sergeant Wrenn, "I believe I can intercede on your behalf with the Tourist Bureau."

"Would you?" asked Janet.

"It would be my pleasure."

"Well," said Gary, looking at Frank and Joe, "I guess that this wraps it all up. How can we ever thank you?"

"Just point us in the direction of the beach," said Joe.

The telephone rang as they were getting up, and Janet answered it.

"Frank, it's for you. It's your father."

Frank took the receiver, said hello to his father,

and listened for more than a minute. He nodded his head several times and smiled, repeating, "Uh-huh, uh-huh—"

"Goodbye, Dad," Frank said, finally, rolling his eyes as he put down the phone.

"What was that all about?" asked Joe, a little warily.

"Vacation's over," said Frank. "Dad needs us at home tonight to help him on a new case. We're going back to work!"

Frank and Joe's next case:

Chet's borrowed Corvette has been hot-wired, and Chet is steamed. But when he tries to nab the crooks, *he* gets nabbed instead. Frank and Joe put the pedal to the metal in pursuit of Chet's kidnappers.

The brothers go undercover to get the drop on a chop-shop ring—and find themselves riding with some pretty fast company. The hot Caddys, Camaros, and Corvettes are burning up the road, putting the Hardys on a crash course with danger. If they don't hit the curves just right, they'll be eating the car thieves' dust . . . in *Running on Empty*, Case #36 in The Hardy Boys Casefiles™.